WELCOME TO HILLTOP

A place to find friendship, happiness, cake and wine

Sheila Starr

Thank you to Helen, my mother, who got her red pen out and corrected my mistakes.

CHAPTER 1

Stella

Stella woke up with the sun streaming through the curtains. She'd have to get some blackout curtains before the summer, or she would never get enough sleep. She did love being woken by the early morning sunrise though; it made her feel that she had a whole new day to achieve things.

She felt good. This was the start of a new life and she was excited and raring to go. Her phone pinged with a text message:

"good luck in your new adventure, love mum xx"

She smiled and replied with a big smiley emoji.

She leaned over and put her favourite playlist on, starting with Nina Simone and sang along:

"It's a new dawn, it's a new day, it's a new life for me, and I'm feeling good."

She jumped out of bed and threw open the curtains to look at the amazing view of the sea, she would never tire of that. She had always dreamed of having a sea view, and now she has. She pinched herself to check she was awake, and this wasn't just a fabulous dream. She had a lot to do today but there was always time for a brisk walk on the beach. She threw on some old jeans and a faded t' shirt, grabbed a warm fleece and headed to the back door where her trainers still had yesterday's sand on them.

When she went for a walk she would usually plug her headphones in and listen to music but today she wanted to listen to the waves and the seagulls and take it all in, senses working overtime – oh I know a song about that! Music was important to Stella, it had got her through lots of emotional times in her life, choosing the right tempo for the right mood had become part of her self-medication, she was sure she had a play list for every eventuality. Today, the music was provided by nature itself and the lapping of the waves on the shore always made her feel happy to be alive.

It was quiet along the seafront at this early hour. It was 6.30 am on a mild March day and the only other people around were a few morning dog walkers that she knew to nod and smile to at the moment. She would get to know them over time as she planned to keep up the morning walks, it was so inspirational and peaceful and really gave her time to focus on her plans before the day's work started.

She used the first part of her walk to clear her head and focus on being mindful. When she turned round to head back, she would make sure she knew everything that needed doing and would have a plan in place by the time she got home. Today she was buzzing with excitement; it was her first day in her new role and she was nervous, thrilled and terrified all at once. She knew it would all go OK but there was so much to think about, and it was all new to her.

She gave in and started to think about her list of things to do this morning and what order to do them in. She had them all listed on her plan at home, but it was good to run through them in the clear seaside air. She was feeling energised and ready to get on with it as she headed back up the path.

She popped into the local bakers on the way home, she had

placed an order for fresh bread and croissants, they opened at 7 am so it was a perfect time to pick them up. She could smell the wonderful aroma of baking bread about 100 metres before she could even see the shop and it made her tummy rumble. She took a big breath in as she entered the shop taking in the sweet scent and marvelling at all the different delicacies on offer in this little shop. It was crammed with all types of home-made breads, pastries, cakes and savouries. She was the only customer and there still wasn't much room to move it was so small. Helen the baker came out from the back of the shop and smiled at Stella.

"Good morning, how can I help you today?"

"Hi, I placed an order for bread and croissants, name's Stella Cranfield" Stella replied.

"Ah, Hi Stella, you've moved into the old house on the hill, that's you isn't it?" Helen asked cheerfully.

"It is indeed" Stella smiled back "I love it up there, such an amazing location."

"Well, I hope you enjoy living there, just don't listen to any of the old stories" Helen warned "it's all old myths and hogwash."

"Sounds interesting, I'll have to find out more about that" replied Stella, not fazed at all. Most old houses had stories to tell and she would enjoy finding out the history of the place at some stage. She knew that it had been owned by one local family for over 100 years but that the last surviving son had decided to sell up and move to London where his business was.

"I'll probably be putting in a regular order for bread and pastries." Stella told Helen "I'll let you know."

"Great" replied Helen "well, it was nice to meet you."

Stella waved as she left the little shop. She couldn't wait any longer, she pulled out a croissant from the paper bag and ripped the end off to eat on her way back up the hill. "Mmmm" she licked her lips, "these are good," she said to herself "I'm going to have to up my exercise living here."

Although she had turned 55 last summer, she was still slim and fit enough, she loved eating but fortunately as well as enjoying the odd pastry and chocolate bar she also really enjoyed fruit, vegetables and tasty healthy food. She liked to exercise but her way, so as well as a brisk walk or a slow run, she would often be found dancing around the house to one of her dance playlists. She used to go to the gym, and she loved swimming but living here in this amazing place she preferred the more natural form of keeping fit.

This hill was going to keep her fit anyway, the steep incline had her having to stop halfway – to admire the view of course. At the top she took a breath again before turning the corner into her drive where her new sign had been put up yesterday:

Hilltop Retreat

The place to get away from it all

CHAPTER 2

Stella

The idea for her retreat started formulating 5 years ago. Stella had worked in Customer Service for over 30 years and successfully worked her way up to Director level. It was a great job and paid a decent salary. She loved the buzz of contact centres and even now as a Director she still didn't sit and hide away in an office. She liked to be part of the team, be aware of the challenges and be there to support them. Micromanagement wasn't her style; her management team knew how to do their jobs and they worked together to deliver exceptional service to their customers.

Over the years Stella became known as a go to person for advice on any management issue. She was always happy to help people be better managers and did a lot of mentoring and training for her colleagues. She loved this part of her job and felt really proud when people developed into successful leaders.

In the year that Stella turned 50, she also got made redundant. The company was taken over and when they restructured, they didn't need her role. Stella was a forward-thinking individual and had seen the signs of change, so it was no surprise when the actual day came that she was told there was no job for her. A lot of her colleagues were shocked but to Stella this was just business, it wasn't personal, and she enjoyed her last few weeks at work.

This gave Stella the opportunity to sit back and think about what she wanted to do. She was 50, she had been working for 34 years, did she want to just go and get another job? No, she decided to do something different. Her redundancy was enough to support her for at least a year she reckoned, more if she was careful.

So, sitting down with her husband, Stuart, they talked it through. He was very supportive, and she decided to set herself up as a management coach. Coaching and mentoring were her passion; she wanted to see if she could make a living out of it. The thought of being able to help people become better managers was really appealing. It wasn't about the money, obviously she needed to make money, but it was about seeing people develop and run successful teams.

Stella set her business up which went really well, she also developed into being a life coach. This happened by accident as often when people came to her for management coaching there would be personal issues that were getting in the way of being a good manager. She discovered a natural ability to help people see their way through their problems and found it very rewarding. After completing some training on effective life coaching, she then offered it as another string to her bow.

Stella had designed a 5-year vision for her business and year 5 was the dream of setting up a retreat where people could come for peace, tranquillity and a break from life. She wanted to offer coaching and advice to anyone that needed it but overall, it would be a place for people to relax. She often thought about what sort of place it would be, all she knew is that it had to be by the sea. She had loved the seaside since she was a young girl and her dream was to have a sea view.

Three years into Stella's successful business tragedy happened when Stuart was diagnosed with a brain tumour and after a short illness, he died. Stuart had been the love of her life, they had been partners for 25 years, they had done everything together and she was devasted. She took a break from seeing her clients whilst she reassessed living a life without him.

She took a few weeks to get herself together. She was strong and confident, but she didn't want to talk to anyone just at that time. So, she shopped online and the only person she talked to was her mum who was such an amazing support to her. Dad had died a few years earlier from a heart attack and so mum understood her pain. Stella was financially secure as her business had been doing well and Stuart had life insurance that paid out a healthy sum, not that it replaced him but it did help Stella decide what to do with the rest of her life alone.

She went back to coaching as she was passionate about it and it definitely helped her when she was seeing people and feeling valued. What she really wanted though was to develop the retreat that had been in her vision and it felt that now was the right time. There were other people out there who would have gone through hard times, bereavements, illnesses, stressful jobs and she wanted to provide them with a place of sanctuary.

So, in year 5 of her 5 year vision, Stella went property hunting in Cornwall, viewing only houses that had a sea view and enough space for 5 or 6 guest rooms, a large living space and plenty of parking. She found the perfect house in "Hilltop". Her dream was about to become a reality.

CHAPTER 3

Stella

Hilltop turned in to her Retreat over 9 months, it was a rebirth of an amazing old house that was very obviously loved and cherished over the years. It felt steeped in history and she had done her best to keep that history alive whilst making a contemporary and calming environment for her future guests.

She managed to get a quick sale on the home that she and Stuart had shared. She wasn't emotional about it, it was just a house made from bricks and mortar, her memories travelled with her. Along with the life insurance and other savings, she had enough money to buy Hilltop, do the renovations and keep her living a simple but satisfying life for a while. She would need to bring in an income and she was confident her retreat would be a success over time.

Hilltop came with an annex that she turned into her own living accommodation. In the main section there were 5 guest bedrooms, that now all benefited from ensuite facilities, a shared living area, a small kitchenette for tea, coffee and snacks, a commercial kitchen used by Stella's chef Marie and a small dining area. It also had fabulous gardens which included a pretty courtyard area by the house that then led to a neat green garden and on into a small wild meadow area. Some of this was still work in progress but it was good enough to start inviting guests along. She planned to build a pool at some stage, there was definitely enough space, but she didn't want to commit the funds to that just yet.

There was also a separate barn that she had refurbished to be used for classes, such as yoga, meditation, art etc. Again, this was all still in the planning stages, so the barn was basic, clean, bright and usable but probably needed a bit more work to make it just right. However, Stella was a big believer that sometimes you just have to start, and not wait for everything to be perfect, so that's what she was doing, starting.

She couldn't really afford any help staffing wise yet but she was not the greatest cook and so she made the decision that she needed a chef to help her at least prepare evening meals. She felt really lucky when she found Marie in the local café. Marie was 40, French and had been living in the UK for 15 years. Her husband left her a year ago and she was balancing looking after her 14-year-old daughter and earning a living. Marie worked in the café 6 days a week, but it closed at 2 pm. Stella was looking for someone to work evenings and so they agreed to give it a try.

Marie had agreed to put a small menu together and to prepare and cook it each evening. Dinner would be a set time and with a maximum of only 5 guest rooms, it should be a straightforward service. Marie also offered to prepare items for breakfast to make it easy for Stella to serve in the morning. Stella was happy with this arrangement as it provided her guests with good food and took one thing off her long list.

Everything else would be done by Stella; cleaning, making beds, marketing, bookings, shopping etc. It would be busy, but she just knew she was going to love this new life and hopefully in time would earn enough to bring in some extra staff.

Her first two guests were Lucy and Grace; they were friends and so were arriving together later today. From chatting to Grace, it seemed they were both extremely busy and stressed out and just needed a few days away to have a rest, relax and recharge their batteries. This was the perfect place for that, and Stella was positive that they would leave feeling happy and refreshed after their 5 day stay.

CHAPTER 4

Grace

Grace was ready for her break at The Retreat. It had been a busy few months with her business and she had loved and lost again recently.

This was a bit of standing joke with her friends. She had met Josh at a business meeting four months ago. His eyes had sparkled at her across the conference table and when he asked her to join him for a drink afterwards of course she said yes.

It was summer and the evenings were warm and light; they went to a trendy wine bar in Mayfair and sat outside on the patio. He was charming and funny; he made her feel really special listening intently to her rattling on about her successes and challenges. He was the Communications Director at a small marketing company, and they were commissioning Grace's firm to put on a spectacular event for them to celebrate their profitable year.

Grace had got into event management straight out of university. She started at the bottom rung of a large firm in London as a graduate trainee. She experienced every job in the firm, or at least it felt like it, over 10 years and then one day she felt confident enough to set up her own business. She loved event management, but the large firm was constraining her from implementing her ideas. She would be forever grateful for the opportunity there and for all the training and learning she had benefitted from, but it became time to go it alone.

She was lucky enough to get an initial interest free loan from her father who was a successful businessman in his native Jamaica. That, along with a small business loan from her bank, enabled her to get started. Graceful Events was born. It hadn't been plain sailing by any means but after a few years just getting by she was now a very successful and well-known brand in the City. She had arranged events for sponsors at the London Olympics, for royalty, for pop stars and actors. This year she would be arranging a Christmas bash for a major star and 300 of his closest friends.

What she wasn't successful at was finding a relationship with a man that lasted more than 6 months. They were either married, threatened by her success, after her money or were just plain weird. Josh fell into the first camp, he was married. He didn't tell her that of course, no, she found that out by accident.

It had gone well the first date, they had lots in common and she found him easy to talk to. She enjoyed his company and over the summer they saw quite a lot of each other. They would take long walks along the river ending up in a wine bar or coffee shop. She told him all about her journey to her successful business and the ups and downs of her family. She learned all about his career and why he loved working for a small company in the city, he shared amusing stories about his upbringing in Scotland. She could listen to his Scottish lilt for hours; he had a very soft voice and he just always made her feel that she was the centre of his attention.

Then as fast as it started, it stopped. He didn't respond to her texts or calls, she got worried and even went to his place of work to see what was going on. He wasn't there but a very helpful assistant explained that he was out of the country visiting his wife, who was working in a mission helping build a school for a small village in Romania. Ahh! That's it, she would give up men and just concentrate on her career.

She would clear her head at The Retreat and share her frustrations with her friend Lucy. She had met Lucy at University and they had instantly become best friends. Lucy was now a film director and as she was so busy Grace had booked them both into The Retreat to get some well-deserved R&R.

CHAPTER 5

Lucy

Lucy often pinched herself to check that this was actually happening and that she wasn't dreaming. Here she was directing a film with Gary Miles in it! Gary Miles! He had been her hero ever since he started his career in the successful boyband, No Limits, 20 years ago. She would have been 11 when she first fell in love with him. He was part of another world to her back then, although he would only have been 7 years older than her. He was the youngest in the boyband, he had a cheeky way about him, and he exerted a huge influence over her and her friends when they were young girls.

Her bedroom walls had been covered in posters of him, there were other bands and singers on her walls, but they were swamped by No Limits posters and particularly Gary Miles. She owned every single, every album, every video they had ever made. She bought his autobiography which she read over and over again. When No Limits split up Gary branched out into acting and Lucy went to see his first two movies at the cinema the moment they were released. Gary successfully transitioned from pop star to movie star and never looked back.

Lucy felt there was something magical about Gary's acting, he became the character he was playing and was able to offer additional insight that would help develop the character and also the story. He also listened to direction and although he would challenge and discuss, he would ultimately go with the Directors decision.

And she was the Director. The film was your typical love story with that all-important love triangle, the tension of who the leading lady was going to choose. It was set in South of England and so here she was on a golden sandy beach recreated at Pinewood Studios, under the sparkle of the spring sun directing her first big movie. How much better could things get?

Lucy spent her young life growing up in Dorset, England, her dad was local there and had lived in the same 10-mile radius his whole life. Her mum was French, her family moved from a small village to the bright lights of Nice when she was a teenager. She loved Nice but when she met Lucy's dad at a conference in London, they fell for each other and she was so besotted that she very quickly decided to transfer with her company to England.

Lucy had always been a creative child; she loved artistic activities and from a very young age spent hours drawing and colouring. As she grew up, she enlisted all of her dolls and teddies to make up a story then she put on a play for the family to watch, but she was firmly a behind the scenes person. When she was 12 her parents bought her a movie kit, it had scene backgrounds, the clapper board and other useful kit for making living room movies. She loved it and spent many happy days directing her toys, and her brother and her friends.

She started her movie career when she took two of her dolls and painstakingly moved them frame by frame. She took photos of each move then asked her mum to help her make it into moving images, which she did. The result was impressive for a 12-year-old and it just reinforced her creativity. It also showed her mum that there could be potential here but, not wanting to make a decision at such an early age, life carried on as normal. It was when Lucy was in her last year at school that she decided she would go on and do Film Studies at University.

Since then she had directed a couple of small independent films which she enjoyed and learned some valuable lessons from. It was great experience and so when she was approached to direct this film she jumped at the chance. She was 31 now and feeling ready, although there were butterflies in her tummy all the time. She could feel the pressure to perform. The team of people around her were very experienced, the actors were A listers and the leading lady was temperamental.

It was going well so far and, although there was a long way to go, she was confident that it would be a success.

Lucy was booked into The Retreat next month, it was her first time at a retreat but she had it on great recommendation from her good friend Grace that a retreat was a perfect place to take some time out and recharge her batteries. Little was Lucy to know that she was really going to need that week out.

CHAPTER 6

Stella

After Stella's morning walk, she got busy making sure the place was perfect, she didn't want a speck of dust or a thing out of place. She invested new 100% cotton bedding and towels, colour coordinated curtains and accessories. She had gone with a yellow and grey combination, she thought it was calming but cheerful.

She set about making the beds, she stuck her face in the warm bedding that had been in the airing cupboard and breathed in the fresh, flowery smell of newly laundered sheets. Then she got on with the job, made the beds, neatly laid out the towels along with the home-made soaps she had bought in the village. There were scented candles on the windowsill, and she couldn't help but stop and look out of the window at that sea view as she put them in just the right place.

She watched the little sailing boats bob about on the waves, all jostling for position, there must be a race on today, she thought. She would have to find out the schedule for the activities happening in the area so she could share them with her guests. She added it to her list.

She and Marie had agreed on the menu for the next few days, her online shopping order was due to be delivered between

10.00 and 12.00 and Marie would be up at about 16.00 to pre-pare everything. In the meantime, there was tea, coffee, pastries and some fresh fruit to keep her guests going. There was wine available if they preferred, she wasn't sure exactly what Lucy and Grace would need when they arrived from their drive down from London.

She spent the rest of the morning cleaning and tidying, she wasn't a domestic goddess but once she plugged her ear-buds in and chose her "lively" playlist, she would dance the vacuum around the house. It burned off the calories from that delicious croissant she had enjoyed earlier as well. She put the shopping away when it arrived and just before 1 pm she stood back and decided she was happy with it all, it looked clean, fresh, calm and just great.

She took a short break to have some lunch, a healthy tuna salad and some fruit. The sun was streaming through the kitchen window in her little annex and she took a mindful moment to make the most of it. She had learned all about mindfulness some years ago. It was during a time in her life when she realised that she spent almost all of her time thinking about what she should be doing and wishing her life away. Mindfulness helped her live for today and enjoy each moment.

She now used an online app to practice mindfulness, she tried to do it twice a day, it was only ten minutes each session and it just focussed the mind on what you had, not what you didn't have. The trick then was to try and live a mindful life which to Stella meant enjoying each moment of the day and being thankful for what she had. Although she had plans for the future, she was very satisfied with her life and was determined not to let it pass her by.

With lunch cleared away and the sunny, calm moment enjoyed, she opened her laptop to catch up on her admin. She checked her social media accounts to see if there were any enquiries. Yes, how exciting. There was an e-mail from a Jayne Massey who was wondering if there was availability for next week. She apologised for the short notice and would understand if it was fully booked but she loved the look of the place on-line and needed a few days away.

She replied to Jayne:

Hi Jayne

Thank you for your enquiry, I do have availability next week. I'd be very happy to book you in for 4 nights on Tuesday. It will be £440 for the 4 nights to include bed, breakfast and evening meal.

I have attached directions, there is plenty of parking on site or if you decide to get the train, I can collect you from the station.

I look forward to meeting you next week.

Kind regards

Stella

She sat back and checked it before hitting send. She wanted to sound professional but friendly and thought she had achieved that. She hit send and added the booking to her calendar. "Excellent, "she thought, "another customer". So, there would be a brief overlap as Lucy and Grace were staying 5 days and leaving on Wednesday. She would need to get used to that, as in time she hoped to have all of her 5 guest rooms filled as often as possible for most of the year.

She knew that the winter would be quieter and so her plan at the moment was to close down December and January and funds permitting spend a few weeks somewhere warmer. That would give her a break and she wasn't a fan of the wet, grey winter days so a sunny few weeks would make her feel good. She and Stuart had loved their holidays on the Portuguese Algarve, maybe she would go there the first winter. Anyway, it was only March at the moment, and there were things to do before her first guests arrived.

CHAPTER 7

Lucy & Grace

Grace pulled up outside Lucy's apartment block in Wimbledon at 9.30 and ran up the stairs to collect her. She had received a distressed call from Lucy last night telling her that she couldn't go away now, there had been a disaster on the film set and she had to sort it out. There was no talking to her at that moment, so Grace had left her to sleep on it and was now at her door ready to drag her away for a few days. She knew she needed it, and now even more so by the sounds of it. She hadn't been able to get any details from Lucy last night, but it seemed it was something to do with her temperamental leading lady.

Lucy answered the door looking tired, she obviously hadn't slept much last night. She let Grace in and with a sigh said, "I really can't leave the set for a few days right now, it's just not a good time."

Grace looked at her and said, "Lucy, will there ever be a good time?"

They sat together on the faded red sofa, Grace grabbed Lucy's hand and said "You can tell me all about it on the drive down to Cornwall and we can find some solutions for you, nothing is ever as bad as it seems. Come on, you need the break."

Lucy smiled at her friend " You are right that I need a break but I am worried that this is going to cost money, this is my first big picture and I don't want to fail at it."

"What can we do right now to make it right or at least good enough to take a few days off?" Grace asked.

"I could….." Lucy hesitated at the thought that was bubbling up "I could ask Gary to try and talk to Layla… but… I don't like to bother him…!"

"Let's do it" Grace was always the impulsive one versus Lucy's very considered approach. The ideal would probably be somewhere in the middle, but they made it work as friends. "Call him now" Grace thrust Lucy's phone at her.

Lucy pulled up Gary's number, she started and stopped it dialling 3 times before she let it connect.

"Hi Gary, its Lucy", she said nervously.

"Ah, I wondered if you would ask for my help" he yawned having just woken up "what would you like me to do Lucy?"

Lucy was grateful that not only was he happy to help but he was expecting it, which made the conversation easier.

"I wondered if you would be able to find time to gently talk some sense into Layla over the next couple of days?" She asked "I am due to be away for a few days and that might be a good thing, it will give her time to calm down before we start shooting your scenes again next week. Are you up for it, she likes you?"

"Leave it with me sweetie" He was awake now and it sounded like he was up for the challenge "I'll have it all sorted for when you come back; you go and take a break, you deserve it."

"Thank you, so much" she breathed with relief "I owe you one."

"And I will collect my dear" he laughed "now go."

She hung up and looked at Grace.

"So, we're on?" asked Grace "let's get you packed and get going then. "She said after Lucy nodded.

Lucy was partly packed, so it didn't take long to add her last few bits and then they ran down the stairs and jumped, laughing, into Graces White BMW X5. Grace smiled at her friend.

"I have music, sweets, water and a post code, we are ready to hit the road. I reckon it's a 5 hour drive so we will stop for lunch on the way and get to the Retreat at about 4 ish, that's when Stella is expecting us. I have to say I am so looking forward to it, we are her first ever guests you know.

"I didn't realise that" Lucy replied "that will be interesting then. I have to say I already feel more relaxed and we have only just pulled away; what a week it's been!"

"Let's get out of London," Grace said, "and then you can tell me all about it, I can't wait to hear about the white witch and what the diva has been up to now."

CHAPTER 8

Lucy

L ucy sat back in her seat and closed her eyes; she relived the last week cringing at some of the memories that came back to her; it hadn't been her finest hour.

The weather had been against them from the start of this week's shooting which already made everyone a bit moody. Layla hated the rain, and she was wearing a period dress that she kept dragging along the ground, it just got wetter and dirtier. The costume department were getting fed up with having to deal with cleaning it, and they were grumpy with Layla which absolutely did not go down well.

Layla was an A list actress; she was the big star of this film and demanded to be treated appropriately; she did not take kindly to having staff being grumpy with her. It was not her fault the weather was wet, and this dress was far too big and heavy for her to keep it lifted off the floor. Lucy tried to keep the peace between them all and, although there was a lot of tension, they had filmed 90% of what they needed to.

Layla was not yet a fan of Lucy's, she saw her as a nobody, an unknown and, as she was a hugely experienced actress, she was keen to give Lucy advice on how to direct the film. All week Layla had been dishing out her advice, some of it was good but it was the way she "told" Lucy what to do that grated. Lucy needed to stand her ground as the director and as it got later in the week her patience had started to wear thin. Layla had also started to feel stressed and had gone off to sulk in her trailer.

Lucy could still hear the echo of the shriek that came from the trailer "I don't care how you do it, just find me the tea that I want" Lucy strode over towards the trailer to meet the shocked tea boy part way.

"She wants green tea, Bakewell tart flavour" he stuttered "I have no idea where to get that."

"Just get her any green tea, I'll talk to her." said Lucy bracing herself for what she knew was going to be a painful conversation.

Lucy opened her eyes in the car to briefly watch the countryside whiz by, then closed them again and relived that conversation moment by moment:

"Hi, Layla" she had started gently "let's calm down and have a chat shall we, it's been a hard week for everyone, and we are almost there."

"Calm down!!" Layla screamed at her "Calm down, how dare you, you little pipsqueak, you can't treat me like this. I am wet and cold, and you are faffing around, everyone can see you don't know what you are doing. You ignore all my advice and now I can't even get a cup of my favourite tea."

"Well, I think you can live without Bakewell tart tea" Lucy regretted those words as soon as they left her mouth.

"I think you'll find it's in my contract little girl! Just another thing you can't get right. This film is going to be a disaster and I do not want my name linked to some shit film" She ranted on a bit and Lucy listened feeling angrier and angrier.

"Well, maybe you shouldn't be in it then!" Lucy shouted at her and left the trailer slamming the door behind her.

Lucy & Grace

"Yes, it wasn't my finest hour." Lucy said to Grace after telling her friend about her week and her final act of door slamming. "I hope that Gary manages to talk her round, we can't finish the film without her."

"Of course, she will come round, she knows this is going to be a big hit and won't drop out now. The diva just needs her ego massaged a bit. Something you will have to improve if you want to work in this heady world of A-listers and Hollywood film sets." Grace had been working on events with similar people for quite a few years now and although she generally dealt with their entourage, she understood the demands they made.

"Now, have a wine gum or three and sit back and enjoy the scenery, we'll stop for lunch in a while."

They sat comfortably in each other's company; some general chat and some peaceful silences while the miles passed by. At 1 pm they stopped at a little village pub and enjoyed a Ploughman's lunch with a small glass of white wine.

"I hope Stella has a bottle chilling for us," said Grace "I shall want to get a little tipsy this evening, I hope you will join me."

"I will indeed" Lucy laughed "I need all the medication I can get!"

After a very pleasant lunchbreak, they continued their journey and arrived at Hilltop Retreat ten minutes after 4 pm. It was easy to find and they pulled into the gravel drive and parked up.

"Oh, look at that view" cried Lucy, she leapt out of the car and walked over to the hedge and just gazed at the magnificent view of the sea and the shore, the waves lapping in the evening sun. "Grace, come and look at this, what a place."

"It is glorious isn't it" Grace agreed "Oh hello." she said as she turned hearing footsteps on the gravel "You must be Stella; I'm Grace and this smitten thing is Lucy."

"Hello, hello" Stella rushed to greet them and gave them both a hug "I'm so excited you are here, come in, let me help you with your things and then we'll get you settled and a large drink, I think?

Grace and Lucy grinned at each other; they both thought what a lovely lady and a gorgeous place, they would have fun here for a few days away from it all. They grabbed their bags and followed Stella into an amazingly contemporary and calm feeling sitting space.

"Would you like to see your rooms and freshen up first?" Stella asked, "Or is it straight into wine and nibbles in my room with a view?"

"Wine, I need wine," said Grace finding herself a comfy chair overlooking the pretty garden and then beyond to the blue sparkling sea. She literally plonked herself down and said, "I don't feel like moving for a month."

"I think I will unpack and freshen up please, I won't be fit for anything if I start drinking quite this early, give me half an hour!" laughed Lucy.

"Of course," replied Stella "Grace, I'll just show Lucy her room and then I'll be right back with the Sauvignon blanc I have chilling; shall I pop your bag in your room?"

"Perfect," said Grace "I'll just be here contemplating life" she watched Stella grab her bag and take Lucy upstairs to the guest rooms. If they were as lovely as this space, she thought, they would be very special.

CHAPTER 9

Stella

S he had heard the wheels on the gravel as the BMW X5 pulled up. "Nice car' she thought. She hovered in the hallway not wanting to hassle them as soon as they arrived. She watched as Lucy walked over to the hedge and smiled as she saw the awe on Lucy's face at that wonderful view. She understood that feeling. She decided to wander out and welcome them, she could help them with their bags.

She greeted them cheerfully and led them into her comfortable sitting area. In appearance the two friends were complete opposites with Grace being tall and dark skinned and Lucy being shorter and very pale. Stella thought Grace was very stylish and graceful, living up to her name. Lucy had a much more smart casual look about her. Grace accepted the offer of wine and Lucy wanted to see her room first.

She chatted with Lucy as they walked up the stairs to her room, leaving Grace chilling in the sitting room.

"What a wonderful place, you have made it feel very calm," Lucy said as they opened the door to her room.

"Thank you" Stella replied "I have tried to make just the right atmosphere for people to relax in. I'd be grateful for some honest feedback at the end of your stay."

"Grace will be the best person for that" Lucy smiled "She is not shy at saying what she feels, which makes her a great friend, most of the time! I won't be long; I just need a few moments to myself."

"See you whenever you are ready, take your time" Stella left Lucy in her room and collected the chilled wine and nibbles from the kitchen on the way back to meet Grace properly.

"Here we go" Stella poured the wine "how was your drive down?"

They sat and had easy conversation about the drive, the route she had taken, how easy it was to find and what a fabulous location it was. Stella got the highlights from Grace about Lucy's drama this week.

"She really needs the break," Grace said "but I am worried that she won't be able to relax with all this going on back at the set. Will you help me make sure she gets the relaxation she needs?"

"I will, it is hard not to relax here, it's so calming, but between us, we will make sure Lucy makes the most of her few days break." Stella made a mental note that Lucy might need some support and maybe a friendly ear to listen to her concerns. Stella didn't want to impose but her life coaching experience could definitely help Lucy through this tough time in her new high-profile role.

Lucy appeared and gratefully accepted a large glass of wine. The three of them enjoyed some general chat and then Stella left them alone to natter whilst she went to sort out dinner. What a lovely couple of girls, she thought. Girls! Was that the right word, they were both in their thirties but to her, they seemed like girls. She remembered her thirties well, she and Stuart had some great adventures in that decade, lots of travels, lots of thrills and lots of fun. Anyway, enough dreaming, she needed to go and help Marie in the kitchen.

Marie had arrived not long after Lucy and Grace. Stella said a quick hello to her when she fetched the wine. Marie knew what she was doing and was quietly getting on with preparing tonight's dinner. On the menu was grilled chicken, new potatoes and a whole pile of vegetables along with a light gravy just to make sure it wasn't dry. There was then a choice of lemon mousse or raspberry cheesecake, both homemade by Marie. She made exceptional desserts and Stella was very likely to eat a portion of each.

Stella helped chop the veg and made sure that the table was laid, the grey and yellow theme continued here, and she was pleased with the pretty look of the table. She didn't like it too fussy but her new central table decoration and her quality cotton napkins made it feel professional but informal, just the look she was going for.

"How are we doing Marie?" asked Stella "Shall I give them a five-minute warning?" It was now 7.20 and they had been planning to eat at 7.30 so that had worked well. "Oui" Marie often reverted to French even though she had lived in England for 15 years. It was quite endearing, and Stella had used Marie to help her improve her schoolgirl French. "Oui, best stir them from their seats and get them up to the table."

"Oh, I meant to say " Marie continued "that I heard an interesting rumour about Hilltop yesterday, it seems the story is that there is a ghost here, I only overheard a few words but it was Hilltop they were talking about and I think they mentioned the ghost was a sad old lady."

CHAPTER 10

Lucy & Grace

The two friends had relaxed nicely in Stella's cosy sitting room and having enjoyed a couple of glasses of wine after a long drive they had both nodded off. It was a good job Stella came to give them 5 minutes notice before dinner. Grace popped up to her room briefly, she just had time to smell the newness of everything, she brushed her long dark hair, splashed water on her face and looked forward to diving into that soft duvet later on.

Lucy went into the dining room to see if she could help with anything but was asked just to take a seat, everything was ready. She sat at the table admiring the décor and as she smelt the aromas coming from the kitchen, she realised she was quite hungry. She poured wine into the three glasses, Stella was joining them, but Marie was heading home as soon as the main course was served. Lucy had popped her head into the kitchen and so had met Marie long enough to say hello and how lovely the food smelt.

She caught sight of the small smile on Marie's face, so she was pleased she had mentioned the wonderful smell of the kitchen. Lucy was good at those little touches, acknowledging people's effort, saying thank you in a very genuine way. Grace would often comment on how thoughtful she was.

Grace, on the other hand, was anything but subtle and as if on cue she came bounding into the room, taking a seat opposite Lucy "Somethings smells amazing" she announced "I'm famished, must be that wine that's given me an appetite" she picked up the little menu that was on the table "Excellent, grilled chicken and fresh veg, sounds good but it's the lemon mousse that is calling."

Stella and Marie brought in the main course then Marie left to spend the evening with her daughter. Stella joined Lucy and Grace at the table, and they ate the healthy but very tasty meal whilst chatting.

Stella brought up the rumour "Marie was telling me that apparently this house has a ghost, she didn't know much but she heard it was of a sad old lady. Not that I believe a word of it, I haven't seen anything untoward in the year I have owned this wonderful place." Stella didn't want to unsettle her guests but having got to know them a little today she didn't think either of them would be worried. She was right.

"How exciting" exclaimed Grace "we will have to find out more, what do you know about the history of Hilltop?"

"I know that it was owned by the same family for over 100 years, their name was Bartley and three generations lived here before they sold it to me last year. Nobody had lived here for years before I bought it.

"Sounds like there might be an interesting story here," Lucy said as she looked over to Grace. Lucy was sure Grace would want to know more; she was always interested in other people's stories. Sure enough, Grace had that twinkle in her eye.

They moved on to other topics and Lucy told Stella all about life in the movie world and about her disastrous week. Lucy was keen to share her bad experience, it felt that the more she talked about it the more she was able to feel that it was Layla that was in the wrong. That would make it easier for her to eat the humble pie she knew she was going to have to eat to get the film finished.

Lucy appreciated Stella's calm approach to listening and asking, she seemed to ask just the right questions. She knew Stella had been a life coach, maybe she could give her some tips on how to deal with a diva like Layla. She would find time to talk to Stella over the next few days, and hopefully, she will have heard something from Gary as well.

CHAPTER 11

Stella

S tella thoroughly enjoyed the sociable dinner with Grace and Lucy, they were such good company. They knew each other well and were a good balance together. Lucy appeared to have some confidence issues to work through dealing with her leading actress. Stella already had some thoughts on techniques Lucy could use and would formulate some advice that she would share if Lucy was interested. Stella felt she would be, that was why she had opened up about it over dinner.

Stella had found herself in a similar situation some years ago when she first became part of the Senior Leadership team where she worked. Jessica, her name was. Not an actress but definitely a diva. Stella had taken on the Customer experience complaints team and was part way through carrying out a major review of the company's complaints procedure, it was a bit old fashioned and cumbersome. She had been working with her team on some new improved processes and they were about to implement them. Jessica had recently been appointed by their Chief Exec to come in and lead on a big transformation programme. The Chief Exec wanted to modernise the business which Stella was very supportive of, she had been trying to push this herself for a couple of years so this was a good result in her opinion.

Be careful what you wish for though! Jessica had swept in, bringing her many years of experience with her from different industries and just implemented what she had implemented for the last 15 years. She knew best, it had worked before, she had the experience and she wasn't about to listen to anyone else. She didn't even find out how things worked currently, what worked well etc, she didn't care, she knew best.

Stella was a high energy person, but Jessica was in another league, she was exhausting. She rushed at everything, didn't have time for anyone and made very quick judgements without enough information. She was originally from a rough area of Essex and sounded extremely common. Stella called her "Trailer Trash Jess", which was unfair really as Jessica had done well for herself and her accent wasn't her fault, but as far as Stella was concerned she was full of herself and was upsetting her, her colleagues and her team.

Stella learned to deal with her but on the day that Jessica decided what the complaints procedure was going to look like, Stella decided enough was enough and she put her foot down. Stella knew what would work and had plans to make it a much more streamlined and digital process, but Jessica was staying old school. Stella sat at home one weekend frustrated, angry, unhappy. She knew her stuff and so after a lot of thought she put together a plan to woo Jessica, gain her buy-in, show her what "could be", the art of the possible and all that good stuff.

She presented her proposal quite formally, she told Jessica that she recognised her experience and successes. She also said that she knew that Jessica understood the future looked different, much more modern and digital and so she was confident that she would love this proposal. She was using psychological techniques, affirmation and positivity to get Jessica to think differently without pissing her off. Stella talked with authority, calmly answered any challenges, gave in on a couple of small points so that Jessica felt that she had made a difference.

It went well; her proposal was agreed and then Jessica proceeded to present it as her idea!!! Agh! Do you know, Stella decided although she was very angry about this, at least she had got the result she wanted. She implemented it and then left the organisation; she couldn't work in that unhealthy culture.

After dinner, Stella made Lucy and Grace a cup of tea which they took into the sitting room. Stella left the two friends to relax while she cleared the table, loaded the dishwasher and did some preparation for breakfast.

"I'll leave you two to it" Stella popped in to say "I'm going to bed to read my book for a bit, help yourselves to anything you need and I'll see you for breakfast at 8 o'clock."

"What are you reading?" asked Grace.

"I'm reading Katie Piper's autobiography, she is an amazing young lady" replied Stella "I like to read to learn, particularly about people and how they become successful, although a good romance doesn't go amiss now and then."

"I love a trashy romcom," said Grace "I think my life is a trashy romcom" she laughed.

"I like a good murder mystery to keep me intrigued," said Lucy "well, enjoy your book and we'll see you tomorrow, thanks for your hospitality this evening, it's been lovely."

CHAPTER 12

Grace

Grace was up early the next morning, it was a glorious sunny day and she was itching to get out and have a look round. She crept downstairs to find Stella in the kitchen preparing breakfast.

"Morning Stella, I'm going to pop out for a brisk walk, I can't miss any of this lovely day in this fabulous location, you are lucky to live here."

"I am" Stella smiled "enjoy the fresh air, see you shortly."

Grace left Hilltop and wandered down the hill and along the coastal path, she breathed in the beautiful clean air and felt the wind in her hair, it was so invigorating. She thought that maybe this was a place that would help her assess her relationships in life. As well as her disastrous history with men, she needed to resolve some issues with her father, nothing serious but it needed sorting before it got out of hand.

Graces mum had died last year, it was expected, she was 84 and had been poorly for a while so it was a relief when she passed away peacefully one night. Her dad had grieved for about 5 minutes and then gone out, found himself a new lady and had married her within 6 months! Grace struggled with this; she knew that it was up to her dad how he spent his life, but her parents had been together for 62 years. She didn't understand how he could just move on as if her mum was no longer important to him.

There were some cross words about his lack of loyalty and Grace had refused to spend Christmas with him and his new wife. It was the first time she hadn't spent Christmas in their family home. It upset her, but she didn't want to fall out with her dad, so she was going to have to get over it and accept her dad's new life and wife.

Lucy was the only person who knew this was going on in Grace's life, she liked to be seen as the person that was "together", no problems that couldn't easily be dealt with. Generally, this was the case, she had a problem, she dealt with it and moved on. Her man trouble was just a standing joke and although she joined in at laughing at herself, she did actually feel that she would never find the right man. Hey ho, they are often more trouble than they are worth anyway.

She picked up her pace and strode along the seafront, smiling at how good she felt just being here; she would come here again she decided. Checking her watch, she made a U-turn and started the walk back to Hilltop, feeling ready for a hearty breakfast.

Lucy

Lucy woke up after a restless night's sleep to the sound of the birds and the sun sneaking into the room at the edge of the curtains. Her head was full of Layla which led to the diva being the leading lady in her bad dreams. She had eventually fallen into a deep sleep and now she was at risk of being late for breakfast. She didn't want to rush so she just threw on yesterday's clothes and would have a shower after breakfast. Fortunately, her clothes were folded neatly on the chair, so they still looked decent. She washed her face, cleaned her teeth and felt good enough to see other people. She pulled back the curtains and the sun almost blinded her, she squinted while her eyes adjusted and took a moment to take in the view.

She inhaled the wonderful fumes of bacon cooking and grabbed her phone and ran down the stairs to breakfast. She hoped she would hear from Gary today just to see how he was getting on, otherwise it would be on her mind all day. Even if it was bad news, she would prefer to know. Then she would be able to get on and really relax into these next few days away.

She wondered where Grace was, probably out talking to someone somewhere; she was the loveliest and nosiest person Lucy knew. She seemed to waft her way through life with ease, making the most of it and enjoying herself. She had this issue with her dad at the moment, but she knew she would sort that out with her usual no fuss approach, she just needed a bit of time. It was such a shame that she couldn't find a nice man, she deserved a chance at love and whoever it was would be a lucky man to be with her.

Lucy wasn't looking for a man right now, she just wanted to focus on her career and become successful in her own right as a movie Director. She had always had this dream of walking down the red carpet at the Oscars having made films that people wanted to watch. If you are thinking "what about Gary?", well Lucy was infatuated with Gary when she was 11, now she was grown up, she liked him, he was a good actor but it was all business. Lucy knew from the media that Gary had a selection of ladies he took out when he wanted company.

"Morning Stella," Lucy said as she walked into the kitchen "the smell of bacon was calling, where's Grace?"

Stella

Stella had initially fallen asleep quickly last night; she was tired after a long day but was very relaxed and happy with her first day in business. A bladder call had woken her at 4.30 and she then struggled to get back to sleep with all the thoughts of what needed doing today. She got up at 5am, did some exercises in the garden and started getting things ready for the day.

She hoped her guests had slept well and that they were comfortable with everything, she wanted it to be perfect for them. She needed some good feedback on Trip Advisor which would help her get the business up and running and get some more bookings.

She laid the table with breakfast accompaniments; pots of tea and coffee, jam and butter, fresh croissants delivered this morning; toast was about to go on and the bacon was almost ready. Just then Lucy popped into the kitchen.

"Morning Lucy" Stella greeted her guest "bacon is so hard to resist isn't it, it has one of those holds over you" she laughed "Grace went out for a walk, she should be back any moment, go and take a seat and help yourself to tea or coffee and a croissant whilst I just finish this off."

At that moment Grace arrived back and they all sat down to enjoy breakfast.

"What are your plans for today?" asked Stella "it's a lovely day, I looked up the racing and there is a sailboat race kicking off at 11.00 from the harbour. There are a couple of lovely pubs that do great lunches and there are also some fabulous seafront walks from the harbour."

"Well, I need a shower before I go anywhere," said Lucy "and then I'd love to go down to the harbour while the weather is good. I am happy to find a spot to sit and watch the boat race and a pub lunch sounds perfect. We can do one of the walks tomorrow maybe". Lucy looked at Grace "What do you think?"

"Yep, sounds like a plan to me, I'll sit and read my book and probably be completely distracted by the view, while you go and get ready, no hurry, take your time unless I can help you clear up Stella?" asked Grace.

"No, no, definitely not, you are paying guests, you go and relax and take it easy, I've got it" replied Stella.

Lucy went to shower; Grace went to sit and look at the view and Stella got on with tidying up. The nice thing about this arrangement was that Stella didn't have to provide lunch. She had given Grace a key and they knew her mobile number if they needed anything.

CHAPTER 13

Stella

As Stella had a few hours to herself today she was meeting a friend for lunch at a nearby café. Philip was someone she worked with in a previous life; he was a Consultant who worked with her on a project and they just hit it off. They both kept in touch with each other over the years and when he decided to divorce his wife and move away from Coventry, he had moved down to Cornwall. He lived only 20 miles away now. He helped her with her website design and was a good friend and today she was keen to share her first experiences at running her retreat.

After breakfast and checking on any enquiries, none yet today, she went and relaxed in a bath. She found some smooth lavender bubble bath that her mum sent her when she moved here and she lay in the warm water with some classical favourites on the radio, surrounded by luxurious bubbles. She didn't have a bath very often; she was more of a shower girl but today she enjoyed it and stepped out when the water went cold, and her skin was all wrinkled.

She dressed in smart black jeans and a casual pink shirt, heeled boots and a warm anorak. She drove to meet Philip as she was going to pick up some supplies on the way back plus, she wanted to be able to get back quickly if she needed to. Philip was already there, sitting in the window seat and was holding a large mug of steaming coffee. She smiled and waved at him and grabbed a couple of menus as she passed the counter.

"Hey You" he hugged her "how are you, how are your first guests, tell me everything?"

"Hey to you too" She grinned and hugged him back "I am really good, they are lovely, and I have another booking for this coming week as well. Have you been here long?"

"About 20 minutes" he replied "there was no traffic and so I got here in no time at all. I am just glad to be out of the house at the moment with all the building work going on. Still, at least it is going on now."

Philip had bought himself a renovation project when he moved down, and, as he was a project manager by trade, he thought it would be fine, but it wasn't fine at all. His original builder was very unreliable, work was done at such a slow pace that after months there wasn't much to show for it. He didn't turn up when they arranged to meet and even though the builder kept making promises he just never kept them. It was a shame as the builder was a nice bloke, but nice bloke didn't get the job done and eventually Philip sacked him and found a new builder. All of this delayed the build meaning that Philip was now living there whilst the work was going on when the plan had been to have it all done before he moved in.

"That is good, are you pleased with the work?" Stella asked.

"I am, he is very thorough, we meet properly every Monday where he shows me what progress was made last week and agree on what is due to be done next week. I get a weekly invoice and he offers some great ideas that we talk through together. It is going to be lovely when it's done, which should be soon after Easter."

"That's so exciting, how have you got on with claiming the

money back from the old arsehole?" Stella asked. She knew that Philip had overpaid on the old job and he had commissioned a structural engineer to work out what it should have cost him and what it actually cost. Since the report determined that he had overpaid by £18000, Philip now had his solicitor communicating with the builder.

"Actually, not too bad, we are negotiating and agreeing a payment plan over the next few months, fingers crossed. Anyway, I want to know all about your guests!"

Stella told Philip all about her guests leaving out any of their private issues and about her new guest that was due this coming week. "each of them has their own personal stuff going on " she said "I am sure I can help them at least a little bit, I'd like them to leave in a better state than they arrived in, that would be amazing and what I wanted the Retreat to be"

"I am sure you can help them" Philip said, "you have an ability to help people without them even realising it, I have seen you in action and its impressive."

"Ah, thanks, I do try!" Stella wasn't great at receiving compliments, like most of us, but she did appreciate the confidence boost.

CHAPTER 14

Lucy & Grace

Lucy and Grace had strolled down to the harbour chatting easily, they had grabbed a coffee from the coffee shop and sat on a bench watching the boats jostle about on the water. They each picked a boat to cheer on and laughed at their competitiveness over the race when they didn't even know who was sailing them.

Once the boats turned out of view they wandered into the village and mooched around the shops and bought a few knick-knacks and some Cornish fudge before choosing one of the 3 pubs to enjoy lunch at. They chose the Sailors Rest which had fantastic views over the harbour, and both ordered a Plough-man's, Lucy with cheddar and Grace with Stilton.

The waitress was very chatty and asked them how they were enjoying their stay and asked where they were staying? When Grace told her, they were staying at Hilltop the waitress smiled.

"I hear there's a ghost up there," she said, "have you seen her?"

"No sign of any ghosts so far" replied Grace "what do you know about that story?"

"Not much" the waitress replied "but old Jack over there at the bar, he knows the history of Hilltop. "Jack, "she shouted "come and tell these ladies about the ghost of Hilltop."

Grace and Lucy grinned at each other as Jack waddled over, he had to be 90.

"Wanna know about the ghost of the old lady do you lasses?" Jack asked in his think Cornish accent and without a response, he launched into his version of the story which goes something like this:

The Hilltop ghost according to Jack

"That house was in the Bartley family for over a century, originally built by old man Bartley at the turn of the last century. His son Arthur inherited it and extended it and made it into the beautiful place it is today. He lived there with his wife Florence. They raised their family there, lovely family they were. Arthur was a builder by trade and made a good living. Florence was always by his side being an excellent hostess at all the parties they held for the local villagers, most of whom were customers at some stage in their lives. They had two children Jennifer and Robert. Robert joined his father's building firm and Jennifer married Christopher, the Manager of the local department store. Robert met Muriel who he was besotted with; he built a lovely house in the next village where they brought up their family. The family still live there.

Jennifer and Christopher, Pine they were, had two children and one day Geoffrey and Rebecca, who would have been, let me see, must have been 7 and 4 at the time, were playing in the garden at Hilltop. It was a warm summers day and Geoffrey was in the paddling pool whilst Rebecca was playing in the sandpit. Jennifer was sitting reading in her deck chair close to them when the telephone rang, with one eye on her children she went to answer the phone which in those days was attached to the wall in the hallway. She was gone only a minute and when she came back Geoffrey was splashing about but Rebecca was nowhere to be seen.

No-one knows what happened, there was a big investigation with the police from all over the region, there was a search, but she was never found. They thought she was kidnapped but there was never any ransom calls and no body was ever recovered. Jennifer and Christopher were beside themselves. Jennifer, well, she blamed herself, you can understand she was mortified and there was never any closure. They spent years paying for investigators to go hunting for any clues whilst they put up rewards and did press conferences, but Rebecca was never found. Christopher partly blamed his wife. Of course, he never actually said that, but you could see it in their relationship. They did stay together but it was very strained, and he didn't agree with how she then treated Geoffrey.

Poor old Arthur died quite young; it was all that manual work that done him in. That then left Florence living with her daughter. She helped Jennifer with looking after young Geoffrey.

Poor old Geoffrey was old enough to know what was going on, but he didn't understand why he had to hide at home all the time. Jennifer wouldn't let him out of her sight, she drove him to school right up until he was 15. He could have friends to their house, but he couldn't go visit anyone else, she smothered him with protection, but it wasn't healthy, and Geoffrey left home just as soon as he was legally able to. He loved his mum, but he couldn't live like that. Geoffrey got a job in The City in London and has made a nice living from trading on the stock market. He is a bit of a wanker but that's no surprise with his upbringing. He had no love for the Hilltop. He told people that it just felt like his mum was still there haunting the place. Jennifer passed away in that house still crying for her missing daughter.

"Goodness" gasped Grace "what a dreadful story, poor Jennifer, I wonder what happened to her daughter?"

"Awful" Lucy agreed "it's the not knowing, that's the worst thing."

Jack smiled at them and wandered back to the bar "keep an eye out for the ghost of Jennifer, let us know if you see any sign of her."

Lucy and Grace finished their lunch chatting and pondering on what might have happened to poor Rebecca. As they finished their lunch a whole crowd of young men piled into the pub, they were dressed in sailing gear and were laughing and joking with each other.

Graces interest immediately perked up.

"Shall we have a coffee before we go for a walk?" she asked Lucy, as she was already waving down the waitress to order.

"OK" Lucy sighed "You know we are here for a break from life, not to go looking for love!"

"It's just a bit of fun" Grace laughed "loosen up, you'll never find love with that look on your face."

They laughed and ordered coffee watching the sailors celebrating their achievements in the race that morning. As they listened Grace realised that the winner was the boat she had chosen to follow. Well, that gave her the perfect excuse to start a conversation.

She approached the young handsome sailor and said

"I just wanted to thank you, you won me a fiver today with your win."

He smiled "You are welcome. The conditions were great out there today and we had a good race. Are you on holiday here?

"We are. We are staying at Hilltop and having a few days away from life. This is Lucy, I'm Grace."

"Hello ladies, I am Jason, I run the sailing school here. Maybe you fancy a sailing lesson while you are here?"

"What do you think Luce?" Grace looked at her "do you fancy learning to sail?"

"Nope, not a chance, me and water do not mix, but you go ahead; we are here until Wednesday, can you fit her in before then?" Lucy asked Jason.

"How about Monday morning, I have a spare slot, we could sail around the headland and have an early lunch at the café there?"

"Yep, let's do it," said Grace "take my number, just in case."

They swapped numbers and with a big smile and a wave Grace and Lucy left the pub. They went for a long brisk, walk along the seafront before heading back to Hilltop for an afternoon nap in Stella's comfy sitting room with a view.

CHAPTER 15

Stella

Stella always enjoyed chatting with Philip, he had a great sense of humour and they were on the same wavelength. By the time she left they had put the world to rights and had a good laugh doing it. There was no love chemistry between them, they were just really good mates and had been there for each other when they'd needed it.

Stella left and popped to the supermarket to pick up a few supplies on the way back. She arrived at about 3.30 to find Grace and Lucy napping in the sitting room. She smiled and left them alone whilst she started to get ready for dinner. Marie arrived at 4.00 and they busied themselves making beef stroganoff and Bakewell tart. Marie was particularly quiet, and Stella asked if she was ok

"Oh, don't ask" Marie replied, "my ex-husband is being a pig, but I don't want to talk about it today, I am too angry, let's just get dinner ready."

"OK" Stella knew that Marie's husband didn't always meet his responsibilities and Marie would have to deal with it "no problem, just let me know if I can help with anything."

"Huh, you could shoot him" Marie muttered under her breath.

Stella smiled to herself, making sure Marie did not see; the French passion was coming out in Marie's response to her husband's behaviour.

Stella heard voices from the sitting room and took glasses and a bottle of wine in to see if Grace and Lucy wanted a small drink before dinner.

"Oh, yes lovely," said Grace "just a small one though, for now, please."

"Yes please" smiled Lucy.

"We have lots of news to tell you over dinner" laughed Grace "we know all about the ghost of Hilltop and I've got myself a date!"

"Is that so?" asked Stella " well I can't wait to hear all about it, dinner will be at 7.30, I'll have to contain myself until then" she laughed and left them to their chattering. It was so nice to have happy voices fill the room, and she slowly headed back to the kitchen that was full of silent tension.

Stella moved quietly around Marie, trying not to get in her way. Marie would tell her what was going on when she was ready. Dinner was served at 7.30 and Stella sent Marie home to be with her daughter, she would dish up.

Lucy and Grace had changed into lounging wear and were sitting at the table with freshly filled wine glasses; they were hungry after their long walk today.

"So," said Stella "tell me everything."

Grace launched into the story of young Rebecca's disappearance with Lucy chipping in now and then.

"Goodness" exclaimed Stella "how awful to not know what happened to her. It reminds me of the little girl that went missing in Portugal some years ago, they never found her either. I think we all assume she is dead, in fact, we almost hope she is cos if she isn't, it doesn't bear thinking about what might have happened"

The three of them speculated and shared their views for a while, it was about 50 years ago that Rebecca had gone missing but she was at the forefront of their thoughts at the moment.

"And, what about this date you've got," Stella asked Grace "who is he, where did you meet, where is he taking you?"

"Well" started Grace "he is a sailor, his name is Jason, we met him in the pub after the race, which he won, and he is giving me a sailing lesson on Monday. He is tall, dark and handsome and will probably break my heart."

"She hasn't stopped grinning all afternoon" laughed Lucy "he was rather nice though."

"Does he run the sailing club?" asked Stella "I think I know of him, he is dishy isn't he, but he does play the field by all accounts, you be careful, think of it as a holiday activity."

They all laughed and chatted about their disastrous relationships' they have all endured at some stage in their lives. They spent a pleasant evening talking and drinking, then Lucy and Grace went to bed early and Stella cleared up the kitchen.

CHAPTER 16

Marie

Marie went home, she was struggling to keep her anger under control, but she didn't want Francine to be affected by her mood. Fortunately, Francine was in her room chatting with her mates on facetime, so she poured herself a glass of wine and sat at the table thinking about what to do.

Her pig of a husband Roger, rampant Roger as she called him, he had at least 3 affairs while they were married that she knew of. The latest was his secretary who in traditional male ego style was half his age and this one had demanded that he leave Marie and shack up with her. "Merde!" she cried out as she thought about it. (that's "shit!" in French for anyone that doesn't know)

So, one year ago, he did indeed leave Marie and shacked up with Claire or "bitch face" as Marie liked to call her. Marie wasn't over bothered about him leaving, the marriage hadn't been good for a while and she knew about his affairs. She had ignored them for the sake of Francine as she was trying to give her a stable upbringing. It was quite a relief when he moved out. It was the way he left and how he treated his daughter that was disgraceful and now she was having to fight with him on everything.

He had just left; he had packed a suitcase as if he was going away on a business trip and he never came back. He texted her to say that he had moved in with Claire and she would need to sell the house so he could have his half! He didn't tell her how he would support them financially and he didn't mention his daughter at all. He didn't call to speak to Francine, so Marie was left explaining as gently as she could that her father had decided to live somewhere else. Francine was confused and upset; she was 13 at the time so old enough to deal with it but young enough to not get why her dad didn't love her anymore. That's how she felt, and he didn't make it easy to persuade her otherwise.

Initially, he made the effort to take her out once a fortnight and spoil her; he didn't involve Claire at the start either which had been good. Over the year it had become less frequent, there was always something else going on either with work or Claire. Then Claire met Francine and they didn't hit it off, it wasn't nasty, just awkward, and so Francine stopped being keen to meet up with her dad. Now, he wasn't making any effort to see his daughter at all. He had cancelled again today, always at the last minute, always something more important to do with "bitch face".

She was having to fight with him about money even though there was a court order agreeing what his contribution was. She wouldn't mind but he owned a successful business and she was only asking for the minimum to get Francine through school, she wasn't looking to make money out of him. She sold their house although the court allocated her two thirds of the equity which enabled Marie to buy a little townhouse in the village. She was now working more hours at the café and with Stella's work as well they were comfortable.

It appeared as though Roger was almost disowning his daughter and it felt like he was deliberately making things hard for Marie for the fun of it. She suspected "bitch face" was behind it all. Francine had been quite upset this afternoon when he had cancelled at the last minute, even though they weren't that close any more he was still her dad. She was grown up and put a brave face on it but Marie could see the tear stain on her daughters face before she had left for work at Hilltop today. That was what had made her so angry. She would apologise to Stella on Monday for her moody behaviour. She liked working for Stella, she was a genuinely nice lady who wanted the best for people. She would talk it through with her, it would put it all in perspective, but right now, she poured another glass of wine.

CHAPTER 17

Stella

Sunday was a wet day and after a later breakfast, Stella left Lucy and Grace reading and listening to Sunday morning love songs on the radio. She went out for a brisk walk; she would walk in all weathers and she found it exhilarating when it was wet and windy. She wrapped up and headed down to the seafront, it really was windy. She laughed as she got pushed along with the wind behind her, almost having to run to keep up with the gusts. The waves crashed against the shore and the white froth bubbled up delivering seaweed on to the sand.

She used this time to reflect on the last two days with her first customers. It had gone well so far, and she was very pleased. She was pretty sure they would both come and stay again which is the best advert you can have. She would ask them to post a review on Trip Advisor at the end of their stay.

She wondered what her third guest Jayne would be like and hoped she would be just as easy to please. Then her thoughts turned to Marie, she was concerned about her after her moodiness yesterday. She knew she had an ex-husband but didn't know the story or what sort of relationship they had, but something had obviously happened.

Marie didn't work Sundays, Stella was happy to cook a Sunday roast for her guests, it was a pork joint today. She needed to make sure that the crackling was crispy and that her roast potatoes were golden. She would do a lovely fresh fruit salad for dessert, she always found that after a huge roast dinner something lighter worked well, she just hoped her guests felt the same.

She walked for a good three miles then turned back and with the rain in her face she leant into the wind and hiked up the hill. She was a drowned rat by the time she got home but felt invigorated. She took a shower then sat in her annex with a hot coffee and did some admin.

She logged in to her e-mail and found a new enquiry. Pete Joseph, he was looking for somewhere to do some painting. He said in his mail that he had passed the place a few weeks ago and thought it looked peaceful and had great views to paint. Stella thought she knew who he was as she remembered a man nosing around when she was doing some decorating, she went outside to talk to him just in time to see him disappear around the corner. He was looking to come on Thursday and stay for the weekend.

Stella replied to Pete telling him that there was availability and it would be great to see him and asked if he needed any equipment for his painting? Stella's mum was coming to stay at the weekend which was fine, and her other guest Jayne would still be there until the Friday. That would give her some practice of having more guests all at the same time and having a changeover next week as well. It was all "firsts" at the moment, and she was excited.

She finished her admin; she texted her mum to check she was ok.

"Hey mum, how are you, how's your week been?"

"Good, how are you? How are your guests?"

"All good mum, looking forward to seeing you next weekend, take care."

"Likewise -smiley face."

She must tell her mum she doesn't pay by the letter on texts, it made her laugh, her mum was quite chatty but on texts, she was always really short.

She headed downstairs to make Lucy and Grace their Sunday lunch. It was a success and they all enjoyed the chat over some good hearty food. Grace talked non-stop about her sailing lesson with Jason tomorrow, Lucy was still hoping to hear from Gary about the diva that was Layla and Stella listened to it all with interest.

The afternoon remained wet and so Stella offered a choice of films for Lucy and Grace to watch. They chose The Shawshank Redemption and they snuggled down to immerse themselves in the fictional world of the prison drama.

CHAPTER 18

Grace

Grace was up early on Monday and had dressed in an outfit that she thought would be suitable for sailing, skinny blue jeans, a white polo shirt with a blue jumper and her blue trainers. She also had a waterproof jacket with her which, hopefully, would keep her a bit dry out on the waves.

She enjoyed a cooked breakfast with Lucy and Stella before she set off. She wasn't sure if that was a good idea or not before going out on the bumpy sea, but she had read that it was best to have a good meal before a day on the water. She was hungry anyway so ate it all and popped a banana in her pocket for later, she was sure to build up an appetite.

"How are you feeling" asked Lucy "you look a bit restless."

"I have to admit I am a little nervous" giggled Grace "about both the sailing and seeing Jason again. Excited and nervous. What are you going to do today?"

"I am going to get hold of Gary, I'll go for a walk, it looks like it's going to be a nice day and I'll try and find a birthday gift for my mum in the village." Lucy replied, "Have a great time, you will enjoy it, it's just your type of thing, just make sure he hasn't got a wife hiding somewhere."

Grace groaned "Thanks for reminding me of my great luck with men Luce! On that positive note, I'm going to grab my bag and head off, have a good day both of you."

Stella and Lucy both waved her off and watched her stride down the hill towards her date with Jason.

As Grace walked down the hill, she breathed in the cool morning air and looked at the bounce in the waves, fortunately, it was a calm day, she would make the most of this new experience. She wondered what Jason would be like, they had only chatted for a short while the other day, but he'd seemed nice. She arrived at the wooden shed of a boathouse in good time, Jason was busy getting the boat ready. He heard her footsteps and looked up with a big grin on his face

"Morning beautiful" he greeted "how are you? Ready for a trip out to sea?"

"Good morning handsome" she greeted in return "I am ready and raring to go, can I help?"

"No thanks, we're just about ready to go. I need to run through a few safety instructions with you, then I'll give you a lesson on the sails and techniques before we get in the water. It looks nice and calm so far and the forecast is the same all morning."

"Great" Grace replied, "let's do it."

Jason passed Grace a lifejacket and tied her securely into it, then he talked her through some basic instructions on how to move the sails and steer the boat. He would do most of the work, but she wanted to have a go at it all and make the most of the experience.

"This is going to be hard work" he warned her " it's not an easy ride sailing, but it will be fun and we will be able to take a breather once we are round the corner and hit the bay."

He was right, it wasn't easy. Grace got smacked on the head several times before she learned to duck under the sail in time when it swung from side to side. It hurt a lot and even though she laughed it off, she was sure she would have a headache tomorrow. She took a turn at steering, that wasn't much easier, but she improved greatly over the two hours they spent sailing. She even got used to Jason constantly shouting instructions at her and eventually started to enjoy herself.

Once they had sailed around to the bay the conditions calmed down, not that it was rough today, but even small waves felt like monsters in a small boat. They coasted to the shore and tied the boat up. Grace laughed at herself.

"Goodness knows what I look like," she said " I feel rather wet and windswept" she pushed her damp hair off her face and looked at Jason who still looked immaculate "How do you do it?" she asked.

"Practice" he laughed "come on, let's go and get a steaming bowl of soup to warm us up, the beach café here is amazing."

He grabbed her hand, her body tingled at his touch and she tried to hold herself together as they sauntered to the café chatting and laughing. Grace looked at his handsome features, he was definitely an outdoors person.

She ate the best bowl of homemade tomato soup she had ever tasted, possibly something to do with the fact that she was wet, cold and exhausted. It came with a large wedge of crusty white bloomer and a knob of real butter. She ate every last bit as they sat and chatted. Her heart fluttered in his presence as she listened to him tell her all about how he acquired the sailing club after the previous owner ran it into the ground. He bought it for a very cheap price, but it wasn't making any money when he bought it 3 years ago. Now he ran a successful low-key sailing club that had gained a name for itself on the south coast. It had cost him a lot; he was knee deep in debt and his fiancé left him due to his obsession with it and not her.

Grace wasn't sure why he was opening up to her with all his

personal details on their first date, but she was happy to listen and for once not feel that she was the vulnerable person in a new relationship. She listened and listened to him talk passionately about all things sailing and couldn't help but smile at his intensity.

They finished up and now that they were dry, warm and fed they headed back to the boat to sail back to the harbour. It was easier on the way back, the wind was behind them, Grace knew a bit more about what she was doing, she got back without being hit on the head once by what she now knew was a boom, and she steered the boat for most of the way back. Jason took over when they got back to the harbour and moored it up expertly.

Grace had enjoyed her day out on the waves and they finished it up with a steaming hot cup of hot chocolate at the boathouse before she headed back to Hilltop to see what Lucy had been up to.

Lucy

Lucy waved Grace off and hoped that she enjoyed a fun day out on the water with her new love interest. It wasn't Lucy's idea of a good day out, but she had never been good on the water, even cross channel ferries made her feel queasy. She would use the Euro tunnel whenever she drove to Europe, much more civilised. She also didn't fancy having to socialise with an unfamiliar man, but that was Grace all over, very easy to get on with and gave everyone a chance. She was so desperate to fall in love that she dived in too early and over the years it hadn't been that successful.

Lucy had other things on her mind, she needed to speak to Gary today. She would go out for a lovely long walk, clear her head and call Gary later. He was not an early riser although there should be some filming going on today. She pulled on her warm fleece and jacket, popped on her trainers, said goodbye to Stella and headed off for a hike. She had a small rucksack, with some water and another of Stella's bananas although she would probably stop for coffee somewhere along the way.

It was a glorious day and Lucy walked quickly to get some much-needed exercise. She listened to the waves lapping at the shore and seagulls screeching high in the clear blue sky. She was miles away in a very pleasant place when she realised that her pocket was vibrating. She pulled out her phone and saw that it was Gary. Oh God, was that a good thing that he was calling so early or a bad thing? She took a deep breath and answered the phone

"Hi Gary, is everything OK?" she asked tentatively.

"Well......." He paused.

"Oh God, what is it? It's not good is it, is she leaving the production? Oh, I know I should have kept my mouth shut, I just couldn't help myself, she was such a cow."

"Stop, Stop. STOP" Gary laughed loudly into her ear, "It's all fine, I was just winding you up."

"Oh, you idiot" shouted Lucy "that's really mean, I've been so worried. What has she said then, how did it go, tell me everything?"

"She will stay on and finish the picture, she is quite an intelligent person, you know, it's just that she has this huge ego. I think she is actually feeling vulnerable, she is getting older now and sees her career ending at some stage. She just needs a bit of TLC and respect for her experience. She doesn't like you one bit, but I told her she needed you and that this was going to be a great movie. Anyway, she calmed down and agreed to stay BUT you are going to need to bow down to her somewhat to help it go smoothly. I hope you are up for that?"

"Phew, yes OK" Lucy sighed "I will have to find a way to do that, I can't have my first big movie being my last big movie. Thank you so much Gary, I really appreciate it."

"No problem, but you know you owe me big time now. I'll have to have a think about how you can repay me" he chuckled "I'm sure I can come up with something appropriate. How is your break going?"

"It's fabulous, the place is great, the location is stunning, the owner is amazing, it's been a perfect getaway, just what I needed. I'll spend the next couple of days planning my approach to Layla before I am back on set later in the week. How's it all going?"

"Yeah, great, as you know we've been mainly filming landscapes and animal shots. I am on set today for some close ups and then back on Thursday when you are back. Well, enjoy the rest of your break, see you Thursday."

"Thanks Gary, yes thank you again, see you Thursday."

Lucy hung up and breathed a big sigh of relief. She had stopped to sit on a nearby bench to take the call and now she started walking again. She walked to the café on the beachfront and celebrated with a hot chocolate and a big sticky iced bun. Sitting there, watching the water sparkle in the sunshine, she felt very calm. She would find a way to work with Layla until the end of the film, she knew she could, she had to.

When Lucy got back to Hilltop Stella was in the garden doing a bit of weeding.

"Hi Lucy" Stella greeted her "It is such a lovely day I decided I wanted to be outside, so I am trying to do some weeding. I'll be honest I am not sure I can tell a weed from a plant but its good exercise and just lovely to enjoy the fresh air. How was your walk?"

"Fabulous" replied Lucy still flushed from that walk up the hill "I also got some great news. Gary called and Layla is going to finish the film. I just need to find a way to show my respect for her and keep it all calm for the next few weeks. But I can do that."

"Of course, you can" smiled Stella "let me tidy up here and we'll grab a......... I was going to say tea, but I think as the sun is over the yard arm we could enjoy a cold glass of cider, what do you say?"

"Cider sounds perfect, I'll just go and brush these knots out of my hair and dump my coat and I'll be back."

Stella and Lucy sat in the sunny sitting room both facing the stunning view. Lucy told Stella about Gary's call and how relieved she was.

"So, how are you going to deal with it when you get back?" asked Stella.

"So, I am going to be the professional Director and I am not going to react to her" Lucy mumbled her thought not sounding at all sure

"What have you learned about Layla?" Stella asked.

"What do you mean?" asked Lucy puzzled.

"Well, we all have our little preferences and ways of doing things, what does Layla like?"

"It seems she likes to have an opinion on the best way of directing, but that's not her job, she likes to be a diva and be adored by everyone."

"Is she a good actress?" Stella enquired.

"She can be amazing when she wants to be, it's just such hard work to get her focussed."

"So, thinking about what she needs, how can you use that to get her focussed?" Stella was trying to get Lucy to see how she could get Layla to bring out her inner actress and perform to her potential.

Lucy sat thinking about it all and what Stella was saying.

"I could make sure she knows that we all think she is a great actress" cringed Lucy "Sucking up to her, ugh."

"Great" encouraged Stella "and do you have meetings to discuss each scene and gather the actor's opinions at all?"

"No, we haven't done that, people just pipe up if they have an idea and I decide if it will work or not" Lucy sat thoughtfully "I guess I could do that; some of these actors are very experienced, even the ones that aren't the main stars have been in lots of films. I suppose they may have suggestions to offer"

"Most people like to feel valued and whilst you will always have some people who just like to come and do what they are told, there are a lot of people who want to offer more, in any job" said Stella "I have seen it a lot over my years working. Different environment but we still had a few divas, we had people that liked to be liked, some who wanted to do it their way, some who just needed clear instruction and would get on with it.

The trick to managing successful teams, because that is what you are doing on set" Stella continued "is knowing what motivates people, what inspires them to be their best, what are their fears and helping them deal with it. You need to lead your team and not bully them. As the Director you don't have to know everything and although the final decision is yours you will get a better result if you involve people, listen to them and make them feel valued."

"Hum, I get what you are saying, I will have to have a little ponder over that, that's quite a change to the way we have been working, but…. If it helps deliver a great movie…..!"

"My last piece of advice before I go and prep dinner, I've just seen Marie arrive, is think about making a pre-emptive strike with Layla. Don't let your first contact be on the set, in front of everyone else. Right, you relax there, I'm off to help Marie prepare dinner."

Stella left Lucy with a lot to think about, but it all made sense.

Lucy knew Stella would be a good person to talk it through with. She started planning her return to the set, she had two full days to get her head straight.

Lucy was just about to go and change before dinner when her phone pinged, it was a text from Gary. She went pink reading it and decided to ignore it for now.

CHAPTER 19

Stella

Stella left Lucy in the sitting room, she knew she had left her with lots of new thoughts and ideas. She hoped she had been able to help, she would love to be able to guide Lucy not just in sorting her Layla issue out but also help her become an amazingly successful film Director by using successful leadership techniques. Now, to Marie, let's see how she is today.

"Hi Marie" Stella smiled as she entered the kitchen "how are you today?"

"Hi Stella" Marie sighed "much better thank you, I owe you an apology for Saturday, I was very grumpy, and I didn't mean to take it out on you."

"No problem at all, is there anything I can help with? You mentioned it was something to do with Roger" Stella asked.

"Mais oui, he is just a pig and poor old Francine is the one that suffers" Marie replied trying not to get angry again.

"How is Francine coping with it all?" Stella was concerned for the youngster.

"She puts a brave face on it and I know she doesn't always want to see the pig anyway especially now that he brings bitch face with him. But he is still her dad and she doesn't understand why he doesn't love her anymore"

"Yes, it's hard for children to understand us complicated adults. I remember when my parents used to argue, it felt like the world was going to end and then suddenly it was all over, and we were safe again. How often is she seeing him now?" Stella asked.

"The last time was more than three months ago, sometime over Christmas and he bought her a lovely new bike and they had a great time together. It almost makes it harder, when he is so nice sometimes and then ignores her other times. Then he seems to think if he buys her something it means he doesn't need to pay any maintenance, then I have to chase him"

"Are you OK for money at the moment?" Stella would have been happy to help Marie out if she needed it.

"Oh yes, thank you Stella, I am doing OK. Actually, with both jobs I can cover everything except the nice little extras which we can live without. That does make me feel better as I don't need his money. The point is, he should be paying for his daughter, he is making good money and I don't want to have to fight with him"

"Anyway," Marie continued "let's not talk about the pig anymore, let's get this dinner on the go. Its tuna steaks, new potatoes and fresh veg this evening, a nice healthy meal followed by Eton mess for you ladies. How are your guests enjoying it here?"

"I think they are having a great time, Grace has been out on a sailing date today, Lucy has had good news about her leading lady and I think being here has given them both the time and space they need to deal with their own thoughts. They are really lovely people; I just hope all my guests are as nice"

"That's great" said Marie "they seem nice and they always eat all of their food, so it must be tasting ok."

"Oh yes, the food is fabulous Marie, I am so happy with it all.

Thank you"

Stella was keen that Marie felt she was doing a great job, she wouldn't want to lose her, not that there was any sign of that but she always liked to praise a good job and Marie needed all the confidence she could get at the moment.

Stella heard Lucy and Grace laughing in the sitting room and took them in a glass of wine. Grace had got back a while ago and had been and showered, warmed up and was now sitting telling Lucy all about her day.

Lucy & Grace

Lucy and Grace sat chatting and laughing in the sitting area when Stella arrived with a glass of wine for each of them. They both had good days and were keen to share the details with each other. Stella left them to it, they could fill her in over dinner. They appreciated Stella's awareness. She was there when they needed her but left them in peace to enjoy each other's company as good friends do.

Grace told Lucy all about her day on the waves and about how handsome and rugged Jason was, she could imagine herself held tightly in his strong arms, a feeling of safety. She knew a lot more about sailing now and understood how passionate he was about it. It had taken over his life and lost him his fiancé, but he continuously won races and had loads of trophies to show for it. Grace laughed about the bruise on her head and how glamorous she looked – not – when they reached the café, but he didn't care one bit.

Lucy listened with interest and laughed at her stories and the thought of Grace looking anything less than perfect was funny in itself. Grace always prided herself in being well groomed and up to date with fashion. She let Grace talk until she ran out of steam and then asked

"So, what did he think of your success in your business then, bet he was impressed?"

"Do you know?" Grace said thoughtfully "we didn't talk about me much. Now I come to think about it, he didn't ask me anything significant about me! Hum, that's an interesting observation Luce"

"I'm sure he was just concentrating on teaching you how to sail" Lucy said kindly thinking he sounded a bit too self-obsessed for her liking.

"Yes, maybe. Let's see, he's asked me to join him for coffee on Wednesday before we leave. Just a quick one, I'll see how interested he is in me then! So, tell me about Layla and your call with Gary then" Grace quickly changed the subject before she decided this new romance was over before it started.

Lucy told Grace all about her call with Gary and that he had talked Layla round into finishing the film but that she was going to have to do a bit of grovelling. She told her all about her conversation with Stella and how that had helped her determine how to deal with it, she had spent some time this afternoon planning for her return.

"So, I am going to contact Layla on Wednesday and see if she will meet me for coffee first thing Thursday before we get back on set. I am going to apologise, tell her that I do think she is a great actress and that I value her opinions. I am going to set up a daily huddle to listen to anyone's ideas and suggestions, we can all discuss them and although I will have final say I will actively listen and consider all suggestions. What do you think?"

"Sounds great" Grace was impressed "I have found that collaboration is the best way to get people working well together and sometimes you have to give in even if you don't agree. You may find you get an even greater production doing it that way. It's worth a try anyway. I'd pay to come and see you grovel!"

Lucy giggled and felt good about her plan. Then she mentioned that Gary had texted her suggesting how she could pay him back.

"Oh Grace" she went red even thinking about it "I can't believe what he has suggested. "

"What," asked Grace "tell me, how bad is it?

Lucy showed her the text.

"Oh my!" exclaimed Grace "do you think he's serious?"

"I hope not" Lucy looked at Grace and they both burst into uncontrollable giggles, you know the type that make you cry and start to hurt your sides! They were still giggling 10 minutes later when Stella called them for dinner.

CHAPTER 20

Jayne

J ayne had packed a small suitcase ready for her trip to The Retreat. She was feeling guilty about her break away but she really needed it and so she grabbed her case, said good-bye to her husband, jumped in the car and drove off before she stopped herself.

Jayne was struggling to balance everything in her life, not that anyone else would know it. She worked as a Director at a local IT firm, the company had grown over the 15 years she had worked there. She oversaw a team of 80 people providing IT solutions for small to medium sized businesses. She was a good leader, her team liked and respected her, and she loved working there. She enjoyed the banter of the office environment and getting involved in some of the big projects they had on the go.

She was very supportive of her team and wanted them to be the best team they could be. She was innovative in her approach to problems and solutions and involved her team in growing the business. In turn, her team were very loyal and hardworking, always committed to delivering great results.

There was always a lot going on at work and they had just taken on a new client that was looking for a technology partner to help them deliver a digital transformation programme. This was the perfect project for Jayne, and she was excited about it. It would mean recruiting some more people to support the programme, ensuring they came with the right skills not just to do the technical job but that fitted in with the client's culture.

Jayne had a good strong management team and between them, they held a wealth of experience and a breadth of skills that made them very successful. They were well thought of within the industry with a great reputation and a bright future.

Jayne lived with her disabled husband. He was in a motorbike accident 10 years ago and was left paralysed from the waist down. That was a dark time in their lives. John had been very active, he loved sports and he worked as a safety engineer in a race team and the accident changed everything for both of them. John took it hard and it was years before he came to terms with his situation which was difficult for Jayne as she was trying to hold it all together. Her company were extremely supportive and gave her all the time she needed to support him.

This last year hadn't been easy as John's health had got worse and he was back seeing the doctors again. Jayne did her best to keep him motivated and took the pressure off him by making all the arrangements for his appointments. All of this had put extra pressure on Jayne who was not only dealing with a busy job but doing everything at home and now taking John to the hospital. It felt to Jayne that they were at the hospital all the time and although the staff there were amazing it was really tough fitting it all in.

Jayne put a brave face on things and although her team at work know what is going on in her life, they have no idea of the emotional turmoil inside. Jayne needed a break and she had arranged for care to be provided to John whilst she gave herself a few well-deserved days off. She told John she was going away on business, which is why she was feeling guilty, but she just felt the Retreat was somewhere she could chill out and have a bit of time to herself.

After the first few miles of feeling bad, she switched the radio on loud and sang her way down to Cornwall. She loved driving and it was a fabulously sunny day if a little chilly in the March wind. She wondered what The Hilltop Retreat would be like. On the website, it appeared to have great sea views and she fancied a few bracing walks to clear her head.

She pulled into Hilltop at 3 pm and was greeted by Stella who came out to welcome her. Jayne was not disappointed; the view was spectacular, and Stella was friendly. She felt some sense of calm come over her as she followed Stella into the house.

CHAPTER 21

Stella

S tella rose early on Tuesday and after her brisk walk and providing breakfast for Lucy and Grace she set about getting the room was ready for Jayne. She plugged in her "cleaning" playlist and made the bed with fresh linen, cleaned the ensuite, folded the towels neatly on top on the bed and made sure everything was perfect.

Lucy and Grace had gone out to the little market that took place in the village every Tuesday, it was a place that brought in lots of local stalls selling specialist goods. It ranged from artisan breads and home-made chutneys to crafted goods and gifts. It was a great place to find something unusual. Lucy and Grace planned on having a long walk and lunch out so she wouldn't see them until mid-afternoon. That gave her plenty of space to sort the house out for her next couple of guests. Jayne would be here this afternoon and Pete arrived on Thursday.

Stella had arranged a Yoga session later today with a local teacher Tina. Stella attended one of her sessions a while ago and liked her teaching style. It was encouraging without being pushy. Grace and Lucy had eagerly agreed to join in, and she hoped Jayne would fancy it as well. It started at 5.30 pm, it was just a 40-minute session and she was holding it in the barn. So, her next job after making sure the guestroom was ready was to give the barn a bit of a spruce up.

The barn was quite basic at the moment, but she would give it a sweep and pop some scented candles in there. She already had fairy lights draped over the beams and some artificial flowers in large floor mounted vases. Once the yoga mats were on the floor and there were people in there it would look OK.

Stella worked hard to get everything looking just right and after a few hours she was happy it was all as it should be. She was particularly happy with the barn; it had come up a treat. She had some free-standing heaters in there that she put on so it would be warm enough by 5.30. She had just walked back into the house when she heard a car pull up, that must be Jayne.

She went out to meet her. Jayne was about the same age as Stella, but she looked tired, she was quite short and although, absolutely, not fat, she was carrying a bit of extra weight. She looked like she wasn't accepting it as she was wearing chinos and a shirt that probably fitted well when she was a few pounds lighter.

"Hi Jayne" welcomed Stella "It's really good to meet you, I hope your drive was ok?"

"Hello there" replied Jayne, she smiled but it was a tired smile "The drive was OK thanks, it wasn't too busy, and the weathers been ok too. I'll just grab my case."

"Let me take that for you" Stella took the case off her "you look like you need a good rest, let's get you in and settled and then I'll make a nice cup of tea."

"That sounds perfect," said Jayne "I am a bit tired, a sit down and a cuppa would be great. This is a fabulous place you have here, I bet you spend a lot of time just admiring the view?"

"I do" smiled Stella "it was my biggest stipulation when I was house hunting, that it had to have a sea view, and I love it, I find it very therapeutic."

Jayne followed Stella in and up the stairs to her room. Stella left her to unpack and went to put the kettle on.

Stella laid out a pot of tea along with some fresh pastries from the local bakery, in the sitting room. There was enough for 4 as she was expecting Lucy and Grace back shortly as well. She hoped that they would all get on, but there was only an overlap of one day and she got the impression Jayne needed some time to herself. She wondered what the story was there and if Jayne was one for sharing or not.

Jayne appeared and walked over to the window. "I'd love to live somewhere like this," she said it out loud but not really to anyone. She turned and looked at Stella "this place is so calming; you have a real gentle touch to everything"

"Why, thank you" replied Stella "I have tried to make it somewhere people can really relax and put some perspective back in their lives. Now, Jayne, I have two other guests at the moment Lucy and Grace, 30 somethings they are, and Grace is quite bubbly. They leave tomorrow but we will all have dinner together tonight. The other thing is that we have a yoga session at 5.30 if you are interested."

"OK, it will be nice to talk to some new people, it will keep my mind off other things" Jayne smiled "Yoga, hum, I'll see how I feel in an hour. I could probably do with it, along with lots more exercise. I have piled on the weight over the last few months. It's all been ready meals and grabbing sandwiches when I can. Then, of course, you can't have a sandwich without a packet of crisps, can you? Now, pass me one of those delicious looking pastries" Jayne laughed and Stella joined her.

"What's all this fun?" laughed Grace as she bounded into the room with Lucy close behind "Ah, tea and pastries, perfect. I have built up quite an appetite walking up that hill"

Stella introduced Jayne to Lucy and Grace and then left them to get acquainted whilst she went and started helping Marie with dinner. She wanted dinner to be all prepared so that Marie could join the yoga class if she wanted to.

Stella

Stella kept popping in to make sure her guests had what they needed and at 5.00 she reminded them that the yoga was in the barn at 5.30.

"I might need a drink before I show myself up at yoga" stated Grace "anyone want to join me?"

"Oh yes," said Jayne "I don't think I could do it without a bit of Dutch courage."

Stella quickly disappeared and reappeared with a bottle of white wine and 3 glasses.

"Not for me," said Lucy "I'll probably be sick doing exercise after a drink. I'll just hope that you lot are so wasted you won't notice how crap I am."

They all laughed, Grace and Jayne supped a small glass of wine and then they all headed upstairs to change into something suitable. They each arrived in the barn in varying types of sportswear, Grace, as always, in designer leggings and a gym top, Lucy in loose fitting exercise gear; not that she needed to be hiding her figure, Jayne arrived in stylish jogging bottoms and tennis polo shirt all just slightly too tight and Stella had her matching gym kit on. Marie who decided to join at the last minute just took off her chefs' whites and was in jeans and a t-shirt.

Tina had arrived at 5 pm and had set herself up in the barn. Tina, of course, was slim and fit wearing just what you would expect a yoga teacher to wear. She had set up her music and laid the mats out ready for her class. Tina was used to carrying out yoga classes in all sorts of locations and with all types of customer, so she started easily with some breathing and stretching before she pushed them gently into some more difficult moves.

Grace, Lucy and Stella followed the routines quite easily, Jayne struggled but kept with it and Marie was hysterical as she had no coordination at all. She kept losing her balance causing everyone else to lose their zen like state especially when she kept swearing in French under her breath.

Overall, the session was good though and as well as having a good giggle they did feel relaxed at the end of the 40 minutes. Marie shot straight off afterwards to finish dinner, Lucy and Grace went to shower and change, Jayne went to collapse on her bed before showering and changing leaving Stella and Tina clearing up.

CHAPTER 22

Jayne

P hew, what a workout that was. Jayne collapsed on her bed after the yoga session. She laughed at herself, she enjoyed the session and the camaraderie of the group had lifted her spirits, but she was so unfit. She knew she needed to do more exercise, but she just didn't find the time between work, looking after John and all the hospital appointments. She really needed to focus more on her health, she knew it but couldn't get the inspiration to do it.

Jayne loved her first afternoon here at Hilltop and was looking forward to a sociable dinner. When she decided to book this time away, she thought she needed to be alone and reflect, or maybe she wanted to sulk, however being with new friends had been just the tonic she needed.

Jayne had lots of supportive colleagues in her life and a few good friends, but she wasn't able to spend the time being a good friend. So, although her few close friends were there when she needed them and she did make the effort to keep in touch, she just couldn't find the time or energy to go out regularly with them. Like her colleagues, her friends understood that she had a lot on, but she didn't think she had really "talked" to anyone about her deepest emotions. She was just seen as this amazingly strong and resilient woman who took everything in her stride, and she did, but at what cost?

Jayne picked herself up off the bed, took a long hot shower and pulled on her jeans and jumper to head down for dinner. She could hear the chatter as she walked down the stairs and made her way into the dining room where Stella offered her a glass of wine.

"Pink for me please," asked Jayne "if you have it?"

"I do," said Stella "I have stocks of everything here, whatever you desire you shall have..... well within reason."

"So, you can't dish me up Brad Pitt then" laughed Grace "that would do me nicely, I don't think he is married at the moment either, is he?"

Discussion ensued around Brad's marital status along with any other eligible, rich and famous, handsome men over dinner. The chat was light, full of banter and giggles and Jayne was feeling very happy and content sitting here miles away from her life.

Jayne called John before she went to bed that night, telling him how boring the conference was and that it was going to be a tedious few days!

CHAPTER 23

Grace

Grace had enjoyed last night, the 4 ladies sitting chatting and laughing over completely unimportant subjects. This morning she was meeting Jason for an early coffee at the café beside the boat shed, she wasn't as excited as she had been on Monday but then it doesn't matter she probably wouldn't ever see him again anyway. She'd just go and see what happened, see if he asked her anything about her and not just talk about sailing.

There was a light mist in the air as she strolled down the hill, she'd always been an early riser, she didn't feel the need to sleep in, just her 6 hours was enough and then she was restless and itching to get up and get on with the day. Jason was the same, he was there before her and had a steaming mug of coffee waiting for her.

"Good morning beautiful" he stood up and gave her a peck on the cheek "I got you a coffee.'"

"Thanks" Grace replied "just what I need on this chilly morning. Are you sailing today, can you sail in this?"

"Not until later; with modern gadgets you could sail in this now, but it's not enjoyable and you never know what other idiots are out there without the gadgets. No, I'll wait, it's due to clear in a couple of hours and then I'm going to head East. I've made some modifications to the sails and I want to give them a test, they should blah blah blah..."

Grace stopped listening part way through. She could see his face light up as he talked but she didn't understand what he was talking about and if she couldn't keep up then she wasn't interested.

It took Jason some time to realise that she had stopped asking questions, he just carried on talking and by the time he fell silent, she had finished her coffee whist his mug was still full.

He looked at her, snapped his fingers in front of her face "Grace, earth to Grace, are you there?"

She snapped out of her thoughts and smiled at him "I better go, Lucy will be waiting to get on the road" She got up before he had a chance to object. "Thanks for the coffee," she said as she left.

She left him there with his coffee looking a little bewildered at her behaviour, but it took him less than a minute to decide she wasn't worth it and he got on with his day. Grace had very similar feelings as she sauntered back up the hill. "What a self-obsessed arsehole," she thought to herself.

As she arrived at Hilltop, she noticed a new car in the driveway and her curious nature made her wonder whose it was.

Philip

Philip received a text from Stella first thing asking if there was any chance he could pop round and help her with updating her web page. She told him she had noticed it wasn't loading properly and she didn't want to miss out on any business. Philip was happy to help; he wasn't a developer, but he did specialise in website and portal design particularly from the customers experience point of view.

He had some work on for the next few days, so he decided to pop round first thing today to help her out. He wasn't far away so he drove over after breakfast, he was quite intrigued to meet her first guests as well.

It grabbed his attention every time he visited here, that view was just something else. He paused to admire it before heading in almost bumping into the door frame in the process. Stella laughed as he stumbled into the hallway, she grabbed his arm and steadied him before taking him up to her annex.

"Thanks for coming so quickly," Stella said, "I'm sure it's a really simple thing but it's not in my skill set to fix it."

"No problem" replied Philip "I'll have a look now; cup of coffee would be good."

Stella popped the kettle on while Philip opened up the web builder and had a play with it. She made him a strong coffee, just the way he liked it and they made small talk, you know, how was your drive over, it's a bit chilly this morning, better than rain though. You know the sort of thing.

"Aha, yes I see what the problem is; that's ok I can rectify that right now," Philip said.

"What was it?.... on second thoughts, don't bother I won't understand it anyway" Stella muttered.

"It was just a setting" Philip smiled "it shouldn't happen again now. So how are your guests? Is it today they check out?"

"Yes, they have been lovely, really great first guests. I'll miss them, they've almost become friends this week" Stella smiled "you might just meet them before they leave this morning, let's wander downstairs."

Stella knew that Philip wanted to be nosey, so she took him into the sitting area and made him a fresh coffee, from the posh coffee machine downstairs this time. Lucy was sitting in the window seat bathed in sunshine with her wheelie case on the floor beside her. She looked up when they came in.

"Hello," she said, "I am not sure I want to leave."

"Lucy, this is Philip, an old friend of mine, Philip, Lucy."

"Pleased to meet you," they both said at the same time.

"It is a glorious spot, isn't it" Philip wandered over to join Lucy in the window "Stella tells me you are a Hollywood Movie Director, that must be exciting?"

"It should be" Lucy replied with a sigh "but its processes are often mundane and dealing with the egos is quite a challenge. Still, it is overall going well so far and it will be great to see the finished product."

They chatted comfortably whilst Stella tidied the room around them, not that it was messy, but she liked it to be perfect.

Jayne came down from her room and joined them for coffee. She and Philip found common IT type stuff to talk about. Philip thought about how different Lucy and Jayne were, Jayne was quite formal in her attire and her approach to conversation but then she was a Director and it appeared her life mainly revolved around work.

"Good morning all" Grace appeared in the doorway looking flushed from her walk up the hill "Hello, I'm Grace" she held out her hand for Philip to shake.

"I'm Philip" he smiled "You look puffed out, it's that hill that does it, isn't it?"

"It is" laughed Grace "I'm not quite as knackered as I was when we arrived a few days ago, but it still puts up a good fight."

"So, Philip, you are Stella's friend, yes? I saw the strange car outside, what brings you here this morning?" Grace asked.

"Just helping out with her web site" Philip replied, he immediately liked Grace. She was bright and curious; she was stunning but not aware of it and she had a lot of energy. Her Jamaican heritage shone through her larger than life smile, bright white eyes and teeth lighting up her dark face. It was a shame they were leaving today; he would have liked to get to know a bit more about her.

"What do you do Grace?" Philip asked.

"I run my own little events company in London, I love it, meeting lots of new people and creating perfect events for them."

"Little" laughed Lucy "it's not like you to be modest Grace. She owns the best-known events management company in the UK right now" Lucy told Philip "She built it up from nothing and is now arranging Elton's Johns party."

"Well, I do OK," smiled Grace. For some reason, she didn't feel she needed to show off to Philip, but.. " OK, I am pretty good at it."

"Tell me more," asked Philip "I've always been fascinated about how those large events all come together."

"Well, it's sometimes a huge beast of a machine, and although it looks good it's often manic behind the scenes with last minutes hitches and problems, but that's what makes it so exciting." Grace enthusiastically described how it all worked and talked about all the moving parts and people and suppliers that it takes to pull a big event off.

She was so passionate, and Philip enjoyed watching her talk about it all. They were so engrossed in conversation they didn't notice Jayne leave and go out for a walk or Lucy and Stella quietly slip away.

CHAPTER 24

Jayne

J ayne had enjoyed her first evening at Hilltop, it had done her good entering into the spirit of things with Stella, Lucy and Grace. She had done OK at the yoga and it had made her realise that she felt better after a bit of exercise. She was determined to have a good walk each day that she was here, this hill would either make her fitter or kill her off, one or the other.

She smiled when she thought about Lucy and Grace, she remembered her 30's well, life was very different then. John was often away working at race meets, sometimes she would join him in far flung countries and they would stay on for a few days and explore. Her career was just starting to progress, they had a great social life with a big circle of friends. She could see herself in Lucy and Grace; young, enthusiastic, full of passion for their respective careers, but now she just felt old, tired and she lacked that passion in life.

She felt very guilty about the way she now felt about John, she loved him, but it was so different now. He had lost all interest in life; his quality of life was poor. For a few years, he had tried to stay positive and tried to find things he could do but he couldn't sustain it and the last few years had been really hard. Then, this last year when his health deteriorated further, he shared with

Jayne that he often wished he had died in the accident. The reason Jayne felt so guilty was that sometimes she had terrible thoughts in which she wished the same.

She knew that was terrible, but his health was affecting both of their lives and she absolutely wouldn't leave him, so she was tied to this life. She needed to find a way to deal with it; hopefully, these few days would help her find some ideas on how to cope with it. She dismissed the thoughts for now and strolled down the hill, the wind in her hair, clearing out all those negative feelings and allowing her to enjoy a quiet walk, just her alone.

She walked a long way in her own little world, watching the waves, the birds, the dogs fetching sticks, the morning mist clear to reveal a clear blue sky and a day full of possibilities. She stopped at a beach hut café and wrapped her cold hands around a hot mug of tea. She stood drinking it at the railing overlooking the sand, she didn't want to sit down, she may never get up again. She felt she could just stay here watching the peaceful life of the beach in springtime. She imagined it would be quite a different place in the summer with lots of kids screaming and splashing around.

They had never wanted children, her and John, their lives never allowed it and she was still happy with that decision. She did enjoy watching children, they could be so cute, but she had never seen herself as a mother. Her sister had two kids and she tried to be a good Auntie but even that she wasn't doing well at the moment, she hadn't seen them since Christmas. Note to self, she thought, send them a postcard and arrange to see them when you get back.

She popped her mug on the counter and started back towards the village and then Hilltop. She would like to see Lucy and Grace before they left.

CHAPTER 25

Stella

Stella and Lucy had left Philip and Grace nattering and had gone for a walk around the garden. The mist had lifted, and the blue sky was shining on the daffodils. Stella liked daffodils; they were so cheerful. It was like they lifted their heads and said "Hello. I'm here" It made her smile when she looked at them, they were a sign that Spring had arrived.

"They looked like they were hitting it off didn't it?" Stella said to Lucy "I wonder what happened with her coffee with Jason this morning, she wasn't gone long."

"I suspect he waffled on about sailing and she lost interest." replied Lucy "The trouble with Grace is she falls for the guys that are good looking and fit, and of course, sweeping generalisation, but they often don't have the personality or ability to deal with Graces passion and success."

"Well, Philip doesn't fall into the good looking and fit category" smiled Stella "he is lovely though."

"Yeah, but he won't get to first base with Grace, he is too old and normal, she just loves talking to people and finding out about them and learning anything new. She is like a sponge; she will be grilling him on web sites and how to give the best user experience to her customers."

They pottered in the garden, Stella pulled out a few weeds and Lucy made the most of the view before they left today.

"This is about the spot that little Rebecca went missing" Stella stood looking out. She was at the bottom of the garden which overlooked the pathway down the hill. "I wonder if someone on that path kidnapped her, it's a bit weird, it would have to have been opportunist rather than planned, and no ransom is so strange. Those poor parents, I can't imagine what that did to them, no wonder the son moved away, there must have been really bad memories here."

Lucy joined Stella at the spot and almost felt the chill of the memory.

"Such a mystery," said Lucy "I don't suppose it will ever be solved now, maybe you could plant a rose in memory of Rebecca in the border there?

"That's not a bad idea," Stella thought "yes I might do that, thanks Lucy."

"There's Jayne" pointed Lucy "she looks like she is going to need a lie down when she gets back up here, that hill is a killer."

Stella laughed "Yes, it's taken me months to get up that hill in one go, and even now I often take a breather halfway up. I pretend I am looking at the view but it's really to catch my breath. I'll go and pop the kettle on. She has some heavy thoughts weighing on her I think."

"Why do you say that?" asked Lucy intrigued.

"I can just see it; I don't know what it is but she is definitely here to work through something in her life" Stella, too, was intrigued "I hope Hilltop can help her."

"If anywhere and anyone can, it's here and you," Lucy said as they walked into the house to interrupt Philip and Grace. Jayne followed them in panting and puffing.

"Give me water," she gasped.

Everyone laughed and sat down chatting and supping tea before Lucy and Grace departed.

Lucy & Grace

Lucy and Grace loaded their car, said their last goodbyes and pulled off the drive late morning.

"I'm going to miss that place," said Lucy as they weaved their way through the country lanes.

"Me too, it feels like we have been there for ages" agreed Grace. "What a special place, we should book to come again."

"I agree, and Stella was a really special person, the sort of person who could help with almost anything. I am now prepared for the next few weeks of filming. I feel like I need to be more myself and less formal, even if I make a few mistakes I'd rather do it through good intentions than being a dictator of a Director."

"That's great Luce, I am so glad you feel like that cos you are awesome but you don't see it, which is good in some ways but you need to be you and then you will be more confident" Grace was thrilled for her friend.

"So, what happened with Jason?" asked Lucy.

"Oh, that tosser. He is just so obsessed with sailing that he can't see or hear anything else. I didn't stop long, drank my coffee, drifted off as he was talking and then left. He did look surprised when I left but by the time, I had walked down the path he was chatting up the waitress."

Lucy laughed "I told Stella I thought that was what had happened, best off without these young handsome twits. What did you think of Philip, you were thick of thieves earlier?"

"He was nice, I can see why Stella and he are friends. He was really interesting, and I learned a few tips about improving the customer experience on my web site. I might use him as a consultant to improve our online presence; he gave me his card."

"Did he indeed?" Lucy smiled.

"Not like that, you dirty girl" laughed Grace "he is far too old, he's semi-retired and lives in the back of beyond. I just liked his ideas."

"Right, you just tell yourself that" they laughed together, two very close friends who knew each other well and loved to take the mickey out of each other.

"Anyway, you've still got to do unspeakable things to Gary" teased Grace "I can't believe it of him, he seems so nice."

Lucy went red just at the thought of that text, there was no way she was wearing that or doing that to him! "I hope he is just winding me up and making the most of it seeing as he helped out with the Layla situation. I am not sure I can face seeing him tomorrow after that."

"Did you reply?" asked Grace.

"I did, "In your dreams" I sent back," Lucy said, "I haven't heard from him since."

"Oh, you are going to have a fun day tomorrow, what with sucking up to Layla and not sucking Gary, I can't wait to talk to you tomorrow evening."

Philip

Philip watched as Grace and Lucy drove away. He was pleased he had managed to give Grace his card and hoped that she would call him to help with her online strategy. He didn't care what she called about, he just hoped she called.

Philip saw Stella watching him and he turned to talk to her before he left himself.

"So, they are all lovely guests, and it seems to be going really well, I am so pleased for you."

"Uh huh" smiled Stella "some more lovely than others I think" she nudged him in his ribs with her elbow "hey hey?"

"I don't know what you are talking about," he nudged back.

"Just don't get your hopes up too much my friend," Stella warned "she is young and feisty and unlikely to fall for an oldy like you."

"I'm only 48" he exclaimed "and a young 48 at that" he flexed his muscles.

He felt young at heart and he did keep fit and healthy; he was full of energy although to be fair it wasn't the energy he had when he was 30.

"Yeah, but she's only early 30's and she is a young 30, anyway just don't get your heart broken."

"Point taken" Philip sighed "I'll just drive home to my oldies bungalow and play some of my oldies music sitting in my slippers."

"Go on with you" Stella laughed and pushed him towards his car. "Thank you for coming and fixing my website, hope your work goes well this week, catch up with you soon."

Philip got into his Jaguar F-Type convertible, his old man's sports car, and sped off down the hill. He wouldn't have been able to afford this when he was 30, he thought, but now it put a big smile on his face. He drove home thinking about Grace and wondering if she would call.

CHAPTER 26

Jayne

J ayne was exhausted after her walk back up the hill. After Lucy and Grace had left and Stella had walked Philip out to his car she curled up on a chair in the sitting room and had a nap. She hadn't meant to have a nap, but she couldn't keep her eyes open. She vaguely remembered Stella coming and saying something, but she didn't know what she'd said as she drifted off into dreamland.

She was walking along a golden sandy beach with pretty beach shacks on one side and the clear blue sea on the other. The sun was hot, and she went and paddled in the water, splashing the water around her tanned legs. It felt like it was her beach, she had it all to herself, not a single other person around. She caught sight of her reflection in the water and liked what she saw, tall, slim and brown... and then Bam, an alligator was lunging at her... she woke up with a start.

Jayne's heart was pumping hard and it took her a few minutes to calm down and remember where she was. She sipped some water from the glass Stella had given her earlier and walked over to the window. She could see Stella out in the garden tidying up the borders, she waved when Stella turned to see her. They were the same age and yet Stella was slim, fit and tanned and very clearly happy with her life. Must be this sea air.

Jayne decided to have a shower and get herself tidied up, she didn't like feeling unkempt and out of control, although her walk and rest had left her feeling quite free and cheerful. Still, shower and change she did and when she came back downstairs, she was carrying her work bag and laptop. She popped outside and asked Stella if it was OK to set up and do some work at the dining table.

"It is today," Stella replied "as there is no-one else here but once Pete and then my mum arrive you will have to work in your room. I don't want to be awkward, but this is somewhere to get away from work and other people won't want to be impacted."

"No problem," said Jayne "I don't want to work much but I do have a few things to get done and if I get them done today then I can relax for the rest of my stay."

"Good," said Stella "because it seems to me that you need a break, that's why you came here, am I right?"

"You are very perceptive Stella," said Jayne "I struggle to switch off though and have a few things on my mind. I'll just do a couple of hours work and then I'll try and relax."

"Great, come and find me when you are done, and we'll enjoy a cheeky afternoon glass of wine."

"Perfect," said Jayne and she went off to set up in the dining room. Stella was right, she had come here for the break and she really needed it but seeing as she was pretending she was at a conference, she felt she needed to work a little.

She settled down to responding to e-mails and updating the latest project plan for the digital transformation programme they were working on. She talked to her senior managers and made sure they had everything they needed until she got back into the office on Monday. Of course, they did have, she knew that, but she wanted them to know she was here for them.

Three hours later Stella came in and waved a glass of Pinot in front of her.

"Come on," said Stella "I think it's warm enough to sit in the garden and drink this if you pop a fleece on."

"I'll be right there," said Jayne. She stretched as she had been bent over her laptop and her shoulders ached "I'll just give John, my husband a quick call and I'll follow you out."

She waited until she thought Stella was out of earshot and called John.

"Hi honey," she greeted him "how are you today? Are you being looked after?

She regretted asking that as soon as it came out of her mouth, as she just got a lot of moaning about how she should be there, and these other people didn't do things right. He did try to be nice to her after he got that all off his chest. He asked about her conference and where she was staying before telling her that his favourite tv programme hadn't recorded, and he had odd socks on.

She smiled at that, she suspected Rita, his carer had done that on purpose when he was being difficult with her. Anyway, she got through the call, told him she would call again tomorrow and went out to sit with Stella in the sun with a very welcome glass of wine.

Stella

After everyone had left and Jayne was napping in the sitting room, Stella went outside to do some gardening. She had never liked gardening but here, somehow, it was different. She had learned a lot about plants and what to plant when and where. It was now spring, so was weeding and deadheading all the plants in the borders. She had bought some new flowers and would plant them over the weekend when her mum was here to help.

Her mum was a very keen gardener and would make sure that it all looked nice for the summer season.

She was thinking about people whilst she gardened, of course, with her latest playlist playing in her ears. She thought about Philip and Grace and wondered whether they would meet again, she thought they could be good for each other. Philip would be a stabilising force for Grace and would absolutely support her in her career and Grace would bring some energy and life back into Philips world. She knew that although he loved living here, he did miss the bright lights of corporate life.

Lucy, she knew would make a fabulous film Director in time, she was such a calm mature person and she just needed to grow into herself. She needed to be confident in her own ability and not try and do things the way others always had. She was so creative and had lots of great ideas that would eventually surface into something amazing.

Jayne... she didn't know enough about Jayne yet; she would give her some space to start with. She was giving off a distinct aura of wanting to be left alone just now. She would wait and gently try and help over the next few days.

At that moment Jayne came and asked to work in the dining room.

Yep, that is what Stella expected, very focussed on work and can't leave it alone, she would encourage her not to work after today while she was here. Whatever Jayne needed; it wouldn't be solved by working more.

It was three hours later that Stella noticed that Jayne was still working. She cleaned the soil off her hands, grabbed a bottle and 2 glasses from the kitchen and went and waved the wine under Jayne's nose. Before she returned to the garden, she went to the hallway to grab a fleece. Working in the garden had made her very warm but she suspected she would really need the fleece if she was just sitting.

Whilst she was in the hallway, she overheard some of Jaynes conversation with her husband and it started to give Stella some sense of the issues that Jayne had. She didn't want to ear-wig so she headed out to the garden and sat in a wooden chair at the teak wood table with the bottle of wine in front of her.

Jayne wasn't long behind her with her slightly too tight fleece and her glass in her hand.

"Thank you for saving me from work," Jayne said, "I have packed it all away and will hide it in the wardrobe for the rest of my stay."

"That's good, it is always hard to slow down but we all need to take a break and recharge the batteries from time to time. I remember from my time in corporate life as Director of Customer Service that it can feel overwhelming at times even when we enjoy our jobs. Tell me about your job?"

Jayne was happy to talk about her job, she loved what she did and in truth, she loved being busy at work. She knew she was good at it and she made a very decent living. As an IT Director, she was earning over £100k and she had a great bonus scheme when they made a profit, which they had every year except one of her 15 years there.

Stella could both see and hear the passion Jayne had for her job, she had obviously invested a lot in her career, and it gave her a good salary and great job satisfaction. She enjoyed listening to Jayne's stories about her team and her clients, the good ones and the not so good ones. It brought back memories of her old job and she completely understood the buzz that Jayne was getting from her achievements.

It was nice to see her bring some energy to the conversation as, so far, Stella had only really seen the tired version of Jayne. She suspected although she loved her job, she did, in fact, need a break from it however Stella could clearly see that it wasn't the job that was weighing Jayne down. She wondered if it was something at home. She didn't want to raise that just yet, she would let Jayne remain in this world of joy and energy talking about her job. That other conversation would come when she was ready. Stella understood that there is no point forcing a subject when the person wasn't ready, it didn't achieve anything, and she did think that Jayne would open-up at some stage.

They enjoyed a good couple of hours sharing work-based stories over the whole bottle of wine then suddenly they started to feel cold and headed inside.

"Thanks for the chat," said Jayne "and for getting me drunk" she laughed "I am going to go and have a lie down and then refresh before dinner later."

"You are welcome, that was a very pleasant afternoon, I better go and help Marie and I'll see you for dinner at 7.30."

Stella watched Jayne wobble her way upstairs, she smiled at this "in control" lady who had already started to let her hair down.

Jayne

Jayne couldn't believe how tipsy she felt, it was only half a bottle of wine or had she drunk more than her half, it certainly felt like it. She managed to get herself upstairs and crashed out on the bed fully clothed. She slept for a good hour then, when she came to, she lay comfortably on the bed thinking back over the afternoon.

She had felt really good sitting and chatting with Stella about work, she did love it and it was great to share that. Stella, it appeared, had once worked in corporate life as a Director, so she completely understood both the good and not so good parts of that world. It was nice to hear Stella's stories as well. The afternoon whizzed by sitting in the garden and it was only once they came inside that she realised how cold she was.

Well, she was warm now, lying here in this gorgeous room. If she sat up on the bed, she could see the sea. She checked the time, ah good, she still had an hour before dinner, no need to rush. It would be just her and Stella this evening and she looked forward to more chat.

Her thoughts turned to John, she wondered how he was at home without her. She was rarely there through the day anyway, usually, she worked from home once a week, but she was always home by 5, then she would log on later on and do some more work in the evening. They would enjoy dinner together and watch a bit of TV. It was not very often he even asked about her day anymore, he didn't understand the role and didn't try to. He never remembered who any of her colleagues were when she talked about them or even her more recently acquired friends.

She understood why and that he had lost all purpose, all interest in life. She knew it wasn't her fault and that it wasn't intended to upset her, but it did. She couldn't help it, he just wasn't bothered about anything, he slept, ate and watched tv, that was it. She wanted more, she wanted to travel a bit, socialise with friends, go to the theatre, all the things normal couples did. She had started to resent him and that was making her feel guilty. Then she always returned to the thought that she would rather be her than him any day, and that helped her put it into perspective for a while. She would make an extra effort and not feel down about it, supporting him wherever she could until it got too much, and she ended up in this never-ending loop.

She really needed to find a balance of having her own life whilst supporting John, she just hadn't found the balance that worked for her long term yet. She was hoping that being away from everything for a few days would help come up with a way to deal with it.

She got up and straightened herself, she knew that all her clothes were feeling and therefore looking a bit tight but she kept thinking she would lose the weight and so hadn't given in to buying a larger size yet. She suspected her top button would be undone by the end of dinner; if yesterday's meal was any-thing to go by, the food was going to be good.

CHAPTER 27

Stella

Stella woke on Thursday remembering that she had a new guest arriving today, Pete Joseph. She was guessing by the phone call she had with him last week that he was an older gentleman. They talked about the art equipment he needed so that Stella could buy the correct stuff. He asked for an easel, so he didn't have to bring his own and some cleaning fluid. She had been into the nearest big town where there was an art shop and bought what she hoped would be the right size easel. She also bought white spirit and a few bottles to use to clean brushes.

She would set it up in the barn, but she was sure Pete would be wanting to paint outside and make the most of the sea view. Anyway, she was going to get up and go for a walk, then she'd make sure Pete's room was all ready for him. She had a sneaking feeling that he would be an early arrival although she asked him to arrive after 3 pm.

As Jayne was her only guest for breakfast she had agreed to do breakfast slightly later this morning, she told Jayne to come down whenever she was ready, any time after 8.00 as she would be back from her walk by then.

Jayne came down for breakfast at 9 am.

"Good morning" Stella greeted her "How did you sleep?"

"Amazingly" replied Jayne picking sleep from the corner of her eyes "I couldn't believe what time it was when I woke."

"Excellent, now, what would you like for breakfast?"

"An omelette would be great if that's ok, and a slice of toast, and coffee, I really need coffee."

"No problem, how about a mushroom omelette" Stella offered "and coffee on its way, you take a seat, it won't take long."

Stella went off to make them both omelettes, they are quick to cook so within ten minutes they were enjoying breakfast together.

"What are you planning to do today?" asked Stella "I hope that laptop won't see the light of day."

"Nope, it's firmly packed away, they know they can call if anything urgent crops up, but they won't" Jayne replied, "I thought I might go for a long amble along the coast, stop for coffee, have a nose around the village and just try and destress. I have some things to work through, so I just need some time to wind down first."

"Sounds perfect and although it's chilly, its lovely and bright today, in fact, you may need some sunglasses. I am going to prepare an afternoon tea today for when Pete arrives, so please join us, it will be at about 3 o clock" Stella invited her.

Jayne finished her breakfast and drank a second coffee before she got herself ready to go out. Stella tidied up and started to prepare the afternoon tea, so she didn't have to do so much later. She watched Jayne leave with her giant handbag and wrapped up warm and then she started sprucing up the guest room for Pete. Once she was happy with that, she headed out to the barn to see how she could make it look like it could be an artist's studio.

She chose one corner of the barn and dragged over an old sideboard that she had upcycled. Another thing she would never have done in her previous life. She had diversified into all sorts of new activities and upcycling was one of them. The sideboard had been left in the house and she really didn't want it, it was old and worn out and not in keeping with her calm, clean style. So along with a few other things she had stored it in an old out-building and then over time tried to make them usable, even though she hadn't known what for.

The sideboard was perfect, she stored some rags and dust sheets in the drawers then popped the bottles and cleaner on the top. She stood up the easel next to the sideboard but facing forwards so that if you were using it you could see out of the barn door when it was open. If it did rain at least this was a dry place to paint.

She stood back and admired her work; it was very simple, but it would definitely do the job. She hoped Pete would find it a useful space.

CHAPTER 28

Pete

Pete was tired, so very tired. He had just spent the last two hours with his mum in the care home. It was draining, trying to keep her cheerful and have some kind of sensible conversation with her. She was just miserable all the time. He had struggled to stay today; he so nearly left after the first ten minutes when he realised what sort of visit it was going to be. Although they were nearly all like this now.

He missed his mum; she used to be such good company, always wanting to know his news and about his family. She was funny and enjoyed a good joke and a laugh. His childhood had been very happy, and he had tried to give that same stability and joy to his family.

Pete had been happily married to Gill for over 45 years. They met at the bank where they both worked in the London suburbs. They both started as cashiers, but Pete had always been ambitious and was aiming to be a bank manager within 10 years. Gill was very content serving customers, she was great with people and loved getting to know her regulars, she learned all about them, their families and their financial struggles.

They had hit it off straight away and it was at the Christmas party after a few drinks that Pete plucked up the courage to steal a kiss under the mistletoe. He asked her out and after that, they became an item, they were joined at the hip. They loved going to music gigs, they enjoyed the cinema and had the same taste in almost everything.

They married after 2 years of dating and bought a nice little terraced house together. It wasn't long then until their first son was born. Samuel was a very calm baby, always smiling and gurgling with joy. It was a bit of a shock two years later when Gemma was born, she was as feisty as Samuel was calm. There were lots of sleepless nights and life became a bit more fraught for a few years.

They got through it though and ended up with two lovely children who grew up to be successful in very different ways. Samuel followed his dad into the banking world working in the Call Centre and Gemma was a travel writer, wandering the globe experiencing different cultures and landscapes.

Pete became the manager of his branch after 11 years and stayed there until he retired 9 years ago. He loved his work; he loved the feeling of being a pillar of the local community. As the local bank manager, he was invited to open the annual fete. He was often a reference for his long-standing customers and helped them support their growing children with buying their first homes through sensible savings and finance options.

Gill had been a stay at home mother until the kids were teenagers, then she started working part time as a cashier in the bank. It had been nice to go to work together twice a week. They had a very settled and comfortable life with great family holidays each year and often travelling around the UK for weekends away.

His mum had always been a big part of their lives and Gill had got on well with her. Gill helped him choose the right care home when she lost her ability to care for herself after his dad died. Pete always encouraged his children to include her in birthdays and Christmas etc.

3 years ago, Pete and Gill went on a world cruise, a 45 night trip to some amazing places. They had a fabulous time, met some great people, ate and drunk far too much and created so many happy memories, and photos.

This was their last trip together as three months later Gill was diagnosed with an aggressive form of cancer and after a very distressing 6 months she passed away. Samuel and Gemma saw her as much as they could, Gemma got herself assignments much closer to home so she could support her mum. Samuel brought his 3 children over often to make the most of the time left. Gill was at home right until the last two weeks when she was more comfortable in a local respite centre. She had some great last memories with her family and Pete was there every step of the way.

She had no regrets, she had been blessed with a wonderful family and doting husband, some great trips and although she was sad not to see her grandchildren grow up she knew they had a bright future ahead of them.

It was Pete she felt sorry for, they had spent over 45 years together, they did everything together and she hoped that he would be able to eventually find peace and move on with his life.

Pete was devastated after Gill passed away and took to his bed for a few weeks. Samuel was there every day making sure he ate or at least drank something; he was upset at seeing his dad in such a decline. Eventually and suddenly Pete had done sulking and one day, he got up, showered and dressed and when Samuel arrived that day, he found his dad in the garage with an easel and a set of paints.

Gill had encouraged him take to up a hobby when he retired, mainly to get him from under her feet every day. He had decided to try and paint, he had always admired good art and today felt like a good day to start painting again.

These days, 3 years later in between visiting his mum, he travelled the UK, finding picturesque locations to paint landscapes. On one trip to Cornwall, he had come across a quiet, small retreat just about to open, where they specialised in providing peace and tranquillity for anyone that needed to get away from their life. He had popped into the garden to see what it was like and he instantly felt calm there. He had booked himself in for a few days where he would do some painting. He was all packed and ready to go, he looked at his watch, he might be a bit early, but he'd head off anyway, he could stop on the way for some lunch.

CHAPTER 29

Jayne

J ayne couldn't believe how relaxed she felt after just two nights away. She still had those niggling guilty thoughts about leaving John with carers for a few days but justified it by knowing she would be a better person when she got back. She really felt that she was in a place where she could focus on herself and how she could balance everything in her life right now and give herself some "me time."

She had been walking in her own little world for two hours before she realised, she desperately needed a wee, must be all that coffee she had this morning. She spotted a beachside cafe in the distance and made straight for the toilets before enjoying another coffee. She avoided the tasty looking cakes and cookies and just had the coffee outside looking over the beach. There were a few children playing in the sand wrapped up in anoraks and hats. She wondered what sort of mother she would have been, she liked children but only from a distance.

"I like kids, but I couldn't eat a whole one" John would always say when anyone mentioned children.

She smiled at the thought, she did have some great memories of their many years together before the accident. It was such a shame that John had lost the use of his legs, it meant he also lost his job, his ability to drive and ride motorbikes and that all led to him losing his purpose and any passion for anything else. They had found some great restaurants that catered for wheelchairs and he did love eating out, especially places that had a decent view – it didn't matter what the view was as long as it was something interesting.

That didn't help with her weight gain, along with often being so busy at work she would snack rather than have a good healthy lunch. Anyway, today she enjoyed a healthy breakfast, she had just avoided a cake and she would grab a salad somewhere before she was tempted by Stella's afternoon tea, that way she wouldn't eat too much of it.

She walked back to the village at pace, hoping it would shed a few calories, she'd love to go home a few pounds lighter than she arrived. In the village, she pottered around the shops including the book shop. She loved books and would treat herself to a couple to start reading while she was here. She liked a good self-help book, not that they were always effective, and she also had a guilty pleasure for a good old trashy love story. She picked one of each:

"Triggers" by Marshall Goldsmith and "Love at first like" by Hannah Orenstein. That would keep her busy for a few days. Once she got into a book Jayne tended to read and read until she had finished so it often only took a few days to read a book. Then at other times, they would sit around part read for weeks.

She had a light salad and glass of orange juice in the café in the bookshop where she couldn't help but start reading Triggers. She was on chapter 6 before she put the book away and started the trek back up that hill to Hilltop. The book had started to make her think about the way she reacted to people and environments. It was all about how you respond to things, what triggers certain responses. It was fascinating and she realised that she had some unhealthy responses to some triggers in her life that maybe with a bit of thought she could change.

She was so deep in thought that she suddenly found herself at the top of the hill, she had got up it in one go without a pause for breath, she was panting but, hey, that was an achievement. She was looking forward to a cup of tea.

Pete

Pete tried to take his time, he even stopped at a garden centre for a sandwich, but he arrived at Hilltop at ten past two. He pulled in and sat in his car wondering if he should drive around the block a few times when he saw a lady come out, he assumed was Stella. She had sounded nice on the phone, very keen to provide whatever equipment he needed for his painting.

He opened his car door.

"Hello there, sorry I'm a little early, an old habit I'm afraid."

"No problem at all" Stella gave him a big smile and shook his hand as he got out of the car " I am all ready for you, let me grab your case and show you to your room. I have afternoon tea ready for 3 o'clock and my other guest Jayne will join us as well."

"Sounds lovely. This is a fabulous spot you have here. I did wander in a few weeks ago, that's why I booked it, it just felt so calm and picturesque" said Pete.

"Ah, yes" replied Stella, "I think I saw you just as you left, I came out to say hello, but I was too late. I am so glad you decided to book in, you should be able to paint a few great pictures here. I'll show you the barn after you settle in."

They walked in and upstairs, Stella showed Pete where everything was and asked him to join her for tea once he was unpacked and settled.

Pete loved the room and the view; he knew he would be very happy painting here. He had two cases, one with his clothes and ablutions in and the other with all his painting paraphernalia.

He unpacked his clothes, organised himself and sat looking out of the window at all the different views, the nature, the garden, the sea and the sky – glorious.

When Pete got downstairs Stella introduced him to Jayne and poured them all a cup of tea. She had provided a lovely mix of small sandwiches, cakes and also some chopped veg and dip, crudities he thought you called them. He noticed that Jayne was being good and nibbling at the veg whilst he went straight in for two sandwiches and a slice of Victoria sponge. Pete was slightly portly and very comfortable with it; he enjoyed his food and his beer and at 69 he wasn't into compromising any more.

"This is lovely Stella" Pete commented "you should try some of this cake, it's really light and full of flavour" he said to Jayne.

"Oh don't" sighed Jayne "I am trying so hard to be good and I am really trying to enjoy these carrots whilst all the time looking and longing for a bit of that cake."

Stella and Pete laughed with her when she then said: "Oh, Stella cut me a small slice, I must have burned off hundreds of calories today."

Pete liked Stella immediately and although he thought he could like Jayne there was something about her that made him uneasy, she was chatty but quite formal, maybe corporate would be a good word. Anyway, he wasn't there to make friends he just wanted to paint.

After tea, Jayne went up to her room and Stella showed Pete the barn.

"It's still work in progress," she said, "but it should give you everything you need, and please just shout if you need anything else. It's very secure so if you want to leave your stuff here that's fine, I'll give you the code to the lock."

"This is perfect Stella," Pete said as they walked into the barn; he was expecting some old run down shack but this was a properly converted barn and had cleaned up nicely. "I will bring all my stuff down here this evening and set it all up ready for tomorrow, that easel is even the right size, thank you."

Pete watched Stella walk back into the house leaving him to his thoughts and plans. He then went and grabbed his case of painting stuff and organised it in the barn, he decided he would get up and paint the sunrise tomorrow. He thought back to all the sunrises he and Gill experienced together over the years. He only enjoyed positive memories about his wife these days, his grief had consumed him for some time after she died but it had subsided now, and he only wanted to think happy thoughts. She would have loved it here; he would paint the sunrise with her in mind.

CHAPTER 30

Stella & Marie

Stella was really pleased that the barn suited Pete's needs. When she had left him, he was in his element preparing everything for tomorrow. She had given him the code to the barn doors so he could come and go as he pleased, she knew he wanted to paint the sunrise so he would be up and about early tomorrow.

She headed back to tidy up the afternoon tea dishes and to see if Marie needed any help with dinner.

"Hi Marie, how are you today?" Stella asked as she balanced too many dishes in her hands.

"Here, let me help you with that" Marie laughed at the unstable pile of dishes weaving towards her "I am good, thanks, in a good mood today."

"Oh, why's that then, what's happened?"

"Well, after Roger's behaviour at the weekend I decided enough was enough and yesterday afternoon I went and cornered him at his office. You should have seen his face when I appeared in his office doorway, his new PA tried to stop me, but I was too quick for her."

"I bet" laughed Stella "what did he say?"

"Well, he was quite aggressive at first, blaming work and lack of time and that he didn't think Francine wanted to see him anyway, all that nonsense. But you'd have been proud of me Stella. I kept my calm, I let him rant and then I just pointed out that Francine loved him, he was her father, she was 14 and if he wasn't careful, he would lose her. Anyway, I persuaded him out of the office for an hour and we went for a coffee on neutral ground, and surprisingly by the end, we were very civilised and came to a few agreements."

"That's fantastic Marie, I am so pleased for you. You must have really prepared yourself for that conversation."

"I did, I took all the advice I have had from you and sat and thought about what I really wanted from him and why I wanted it. I started with the end in mind, as you so often tell me. When I did think about it I realised that this is literally all about Francine. I had to put my anger and hurt to one side and if I had to pander to him so be it. I think by the end of our conversation he too had realised that this wasn't about us anymore, it was only about our daughter. He has agreed to keep paying the maintenance determined by the court until she is 18, he will see her once a fortnight and that for now, Claire won't be there, that can be reviewed over time" Marie sighed. Stella could see the relief on her face.

"By the time I left him we actually both felt good about it and I hope that we can keep that civilised relationship going now" Marie continued "Francine was over the moon and they are meeting up this weekend and going for a cycle ride together."

Stella was so pleased for Marie, she suspected the conversation hadn't gone quite as easily as Marie was telling her but that didn't matter, it was a great result. The two of them started preparing dinner, chatting away about the new guests.

Stella was realising that not all of her guests would be as easy going as Lucy and Grace had been, they had got her off to a great start. Her new two guests were much more formal guests as opposed to feeling like friends. Not that Jayne and Pete were diffi-cult by any means, they were just guests.

Stella left Marie cooking whilst she went and laid the table, opened a couple of bottles of wine and then popped upstairs to tidy herself up before dinner. She gave Pete and Jayne a ten minute warning before dinner which was a good job, as Jayne had become so engrossed in her book that she had lost track of time, and Stella had found Pete still in the barn faffing about with paints.

Pete

Pete was surprised to hear Stella's ten-minute warning shout that dinner was almost ready. He had enjoyed sorting all of his kit out and was planning on where to paint the sunrise from to-morrow, he thought he knew now. He rushed back to his room and freshened up and was back in the dining room just as dinner was served at the table.

It was a lovely room and he gratefully accepted a glass of red wine. He was more of a beer man really, but a glass of wine felt right at the dinner table. The food looked and smelt amazing, it was a lamb casserole with some chunky bread, real butter and fresh veg. Just right for this chilly spring evening.

"How long has it taken you to get this place just as you want it? Pete asked Stella "It looks all so fresh and new."

"Well, I have owned it for a year, and it took about 9 months to do the work after I found a great local builder. It has been a la-bour of love and I am really pleased with it. Still a few things to get done but nothing urgent" Stella replied.

"You have done a great job," Pete said "I am doing a bit of dec-orating on my place, it's well overdue but I haven't felt ready until now. It's like I am painting my Gill out of my home, but she would have been the first to say how drab it is looking."

"Is Gill your wife?" asked Jayne enjoying a second glass of rose.

"She was my wife, my friend and my life," said Pete.

"Tell us about her," said Stella encouraging Pete to open up about his late wife

"She was my soulmate, we met almost 50 years ago at work and we fell in love and married and had two amazing children. We had the same interests, the same sense of humour, we loved to go out and eat and we really enjoyed our holidays, in fact, we had just returned from a world cruise when she was diagnosed with cancer. I am so grateful we got that last trip in; it was a trip of a lifetime and I have great memories that I keep with me."

"Sounds amazing," said Jayne "I always fancied a cruise, but John was never keen, he felt that it would be too restricted, who did you travel with?"

"We went all out and booked with Cunard, we decided that we had earned it and I used some of the lump sum from my pension to pay for it. I do understand why people feel restricted and especially when you are young and fit it's great to be free to do your own thing but as you get older it's just nice to feel safe and looked after. The service, the food, the entertainment was all fabulous and we went places we would never have gone to on a holiday."

The three of them continued to talk about cruises and holidays, where they had been, their favourite trips and least favourite, they shared funny stories and lovely stories about their partners. Pete learned that Stella completely understood his loss as she herself had lost her husband, Stuart from a brain tumour.

"How did you cope when your husband died?" Pete asked.

"Day by day" replied Stella "as you know it's so hard when they pass away quickly, there is no time to get used to the idea. He was in so much pain in his last couple of weeks that there was an element of relief at the end, followed very quickly by feeling guilty. My mum was amazing, she was there for me every step of the way and after a few weeks, I started picking up bits of my life again. It was hard but life goes on and I was only early 50's. How do you cope Pete, you and Gill were together for a long time?"

"We were, that's what made it so hard, it was like losing part of me. I took to my bed for a few weeks, wouldn't see anyone or do anything. My son was my rock, every day he turned up, made me at least drink something even when I wouldn't eat. I don't know what happened but one day I just woke up and decided I couldn't go on like this. I had visions of Gill shouting down at me to get up and do something useful. I smiled for the first time since she died at that thought, I got up and had a shower, I washed the grief away, made some toast and then went into the garage and found my paints."

"Is that when you started painting?" asked Stella.

"Gill had persuaded me into it when I retired, and I'd given it a go but that day I decided I was going to start painting again and it's given me a new lease of life. I joined an art class where I have met some new friends and have travelled around the UK finding places to paint, it's been really great therapy. My son was so surprised that day when he came round and didn't find me in bed, I think he panicked wondering what had happened until he found me covered in paint in the garden. Anyway, life has been good since the. I still miss her desperately but now I just remember all the great times we had. Have you got a significant other Jayne?" Pete asked. "I have" replied Jayne, she had to decide how much she wanted to share " his name is John and he used to be in the racing world but after an accident, he is now paralysed from the waist down and things are a bit challenging."

Pete and Stella, at exactly the same time, expressed their sympathy "Goodness, so sorry to hear that."

"That must be hard for both of you," Stella said.

"It can be, sometimes" Jayne replied very matter of fact "You get used to it, you just have to deal with it don't you, the same way you two deal with your loss and grief, it's very similar. Life goes on and you adjust accordingly."

Pete felt really bad for Jayne's situation and was sorry he had asked the question. He wasn't comfortable asking personal questions and he had the distinct impression that Jayne either really was dealing with it fine or that she didn't want to share her personal challenges with them. He changed the subject.

"So, Jayne, having been here a couple of days where would you recommend for a nice hot coffee and sticky bun?"

Jayne and Stella both gave Pete their recommendations and he excused himself for the evening.

"I am going to take a cup of tea up to bed if that's OK. I'd like to call my son and have an early night. It will be an early start tomorrow if I want to paint that sunrise, good night ladies, thanks for your company."

"Night Pete."

CHAPTER 31

Jayne

J ayne felt a bit bad that she had been quite short in her answer to Pete's question about John, but she wasn't one to share her challenges especially with a stranger. She helped Stella clear the table and then whilst Stella loaded the dishwasher Jayne poured herself a third glass of wine and went and sat in the comfortable sitting room. She had brought her book down with her and started reading it again, but she couldn't concentrate on it and she soon put it down on the little coffee table beside her.

She was lost in thought when Stella joined her with glass in hand.

"Ah, Triggers" Stella spotted the book on the table "one of my favourites. So simple and yet so effective, but definitely not easy. What made you choose that book?"

"I love a good self-help book" Jayne replied, "trouble is they only help if you actually action it and I always seem to be too busy to do the actions."

"Oh, that old chestnut hey?" Stella smiled kindly at Jayne. Stella knew from her coaching that time was often the excuse that changes don't happen, that or money. She wanted to help Jayne and it might need a bit of tough love to do it.

Jayne smiled back, "Yep, that old excuse. I use it a lot and have started to realise that I am going to have to find the time and capacity to make some changes or else I am going to go mad."

"Tell me," Stella asked, "what's on your mind?"

"Where do I start?" Jayne sighed and glugged some wine, she was feeling very vulnerable after a few glasses of wine and a willing ear to listen.

Stella waited, she didn't think Jayne really needed an answer to that question, so she just sat back and let Jayne take her time.

"I guess I feel that my life is not my own, that I am treading water and that sometimes I am so tired that I just sink. I know it's not a bad life and I get cross with myself for expecting more but I can't keep that feeling at bay, that feeling that there is more to see, to do, to learn, to achieve. I have a great job, a decent salary, a nice house, a loving husband in his own way, some good friends, that I don't see often enough.

I have had some fantastic experiences in my life so far, I am 55 years old, maybe I should just settle for what I've got but I seem to want more."

Jayne paused; Stella waited. When she didn't start again Stella prompted "What would more look like?"

Jayne hesitated before she answered.

"More…. would look like less time in hospitals, more time spent with friends, going on holiday, not tip toeing around people's moods, not doing everything: working, cleaning, shopping, gardening, collecting medication, taking John to appointments, AND not just the doing but the thinking about it all, making sure I know when the medication needs reordering, when the appointments are and planning everything around them. More would look like me having the time to exercise, to eat better, to watch less tv……."

Jayne paused, there was something on the tip of her tongue that she hadn't said out loud before

"More would mean being single" she blurted out then went very red in the face and explained "I am not sure if I mean that but there are definitely days when that's what I dream of. I love John, I really do but he is not the same man and we don't have the same life that we used to have. I think what frustrates me is that he could do more to help himself, he could participate in life more, but he doesn't. I know his life isn't easy and I understand that he is depressed and I know I have to support him and I do, but deep down there is a part of me that is angry with him for not wanting to be better. He doesn't do the exercises he has been given, he doesn't try to remember his own appointments, he just doesn't care anymore, and he basically sits and watches tv. Sometimes I feel it would have been better if he had died in that accident."

Jayne ran out of steam at that point, and Stella left time and space for Jayne to process what she had said. Stella felt that Jayne hadn't intended to say all of that, but the pressure had been building and the alcohol had let her open up.

Jayne looked at Stella and with a smile said, "Do you think I could have a cup of coffee?"

"Of course," Stella said, "then we can break all this down a bit and see what you can do to make some small changes that will help you feel better about life, don't go anywhere."

Jayne stood up and wandered over to the window, it was too dark to see the view, but she could see lights down at the harbour and it still looked pretty, even at night. She suddenly felt drained. Having opened up to Stella like that she felt the pressure had been lifted but it left her tired. However, now she had started, she wanted to let Stella help her put some plans in place. From reading Triggers and thinking things through over the last couple of days she already knew she needed to do some things differently and she was grateful to Stella for being there to help.

She turned when she heard Stella return with the coffee and gratefully took it and hugged the mug.

"So" started Stella "what would be one small thing that you could do to give you more time for yourself?"

"I could get a cleaner. I have thought that before, but John doesn't like them being in the house for two hours each week but hey, he'll have to live with it. Done – I'll get a cleaner sorted next week."

"Great," said Stella "well, that was easy. What will you do with those two hours that you would have spent cleaning?"

"I think, at the moment, I really need to get some exercise so maybe I'll book a class each week."

"Maybe??" Stella asked, "what's going to make you go and do that class?"

"Actually, I have a friend that does a Pilates class each week, I'll go with her, that way I can do exercise, see my friend and I'll feel like I'm letting her down if I don't go" Jayne replied.

"Excellent" Stella smiled, she could see that Jayne was desperate to make big changes, but small changes are easier to stick to and usually once you start making small changes bigger ones follow.

"If you can just stick to those two small changes" advised Stella "you will start to see light at the end of the tunnel. You will start the momentum, but you must do those two changes to start to feel different. Now, tell me about John."

Jayne told Stella all about how John was the love of her life. They met at a racetrack when she had been bought an experience day and he was the safety tutor. They had clicked immediately; she stayed on at the end of the day and they chatted over coffee. In the following ten years, they enjoyed many experiences of travel and excitement, lots of high-octane adventures and then John had been racing a motorbike around a circuit when he lost it and crashed into the barriers.

"That was the worst day of my life" Jayne explained "I was at the track that day, watching, and when the red flag came out, I watched all the riders come back except John. The officials red flag at the smallest of incidents on those track days, so I didn't think too much of it but then one of the medical staff came to me and rushed me to the ambulance. John was in a bad way, his leathers were shredded, there was blood everywhere, or that's how it looked to me. He had hit his head and was unconscious as they sped towards the hospital. After a few days, he came out of the coma to learn that he was paralysed from the waist down. He was in the hospital for 6 months whilst they operated on various parts of him and then rehabilitated him to be able to look after himself.

In the meantime, I had some adaptions made at home so that he could be as independent as possible. Initially, it was hard, you can imagine how down he was, after being a thrill seeking adventurer, he now couldn't walk or drive. Then over the next few years, he did try to do more, and he got used to the power wheelchair, but he couldn't sustain it. He has just never really accepted his new life and then when he got an infection a few months ago, it dragged him down and now he is not in a good place.

He tries to be interested in my life and on a good day we have a laugh and don't get me wrong, he is not nasty or anything, he can be good company and most of the time its fine. It's just that its very passive."

Stella listened with interest and then asked, "So, is there anything you can do to make his life better?"

"Well, I try all the time, I try and persuade him to play games to keep his brain active, I encourage him to do his exercises but, in the end, it just feels like I am nagging and he just gets cross with me. So, I stop, and I just make sure he has what he needs to make his life comfortable."

"And is he grateful for that?"

"Yes, he often tells me that he appreciates what I do, and he does understand what I am trying to help with, but he doesn't need it."

"OK, so what is he telling you?" Stella prompted.

"That he is OK and that I should stop nagging him?" Jayne realised.

"I think so yes" Stella said "it sounds like you are trying to get him to do what you want him to do and be what you want him to be and not what he wants. That's never going to work. You need to get your head around the fact that he has chosen how to cope with his life. He has a choice, and this is what he has chosen. What you can do is find a way to deal with that environment so that you support and love him whilst enjoying your own choices.

"My advice would be not to try and change too much at once, get your cleaner, do your exercise class and stop expecting John to be better, just accept him for who he is."

"Yes, you are right" Jayne agreed "I know that when I "nag" it just creates a tension between us. It's going to be hard, but I will put my mind to it and see how it goes. Thank you, Stella, this conversation has been really helpful."

"My pleasure, just glad to be able to help you work through it. Now we better get some sleep, it's almost 1 am."

"Goodness, is it?" Jayne hadn't realised it had got so late. She felt guilty for keeping Stella up but in herself, she felt like she had a new life ahead of her. As she walked up the stairs, she realised that she hadn't rung John today, oops.

CHAPTER 32

Pete

P ete enjoyed his dinner but didn't want to hang around to participate in the girly chat, so he headed off to his room and continued planning his painting. There were so many different views he could paint here but he only had a few days so he would focus on two, one of the sunrise over the sea and one of the harbour.

He vaguely heard Jayne come upstairs to go to her room, it felt late but he didn't check his clock. He drifted back to sleep and woke with a start when his alarm went off at 5.30. Sunrise was officially 6.12 this morning according to the BBC weather records. He got out of bed quietly, got dressed and crept downstairs. He didn't want to disturb anyone so he went straight to the barn, he would grab a cup of tea when Stella was up and about.

He was lucky, it was a crisp, clear morning with a light sea mist hovering over the water. He carried the easel out of the barn and down to the edge of the garden where he set up. It took him three trips to get everything he needed from the barn and over to his spot in the garden. Once he was ready, he took a moment, stepped back and admired the view. He smiled, this should be a perfect scene, he just hoped he would do it justice.

By 5.50 he had started painting, he tended to paint the outline and dot colours on the paper so he would remember what he was painting. The sunrise would happen quickly, and he would need to have a picture in his head so he knew how it would look when finished. His son had tried to persuade him to take a photo and paint from that, but Pete was old school and he wanted to paint from real life. Also, he felt that the picture then took on a life of its own and it became a Pete original.

He had been painting for a few years now and was able to get the main outline painted pretty quickly, then he would spend the rest of the day refining it and probably even a second day to get it how he wanted it. Some paintings he went back to a while later and added to them until they felt right.

He jumped when Stella arrived at his side with a hot cup of tea and a warm croissant.

"I thought you might like something to warm you up," she said peering over his shoulder at the painting "that looks great Pete. I might have to commission you to paint Hilltop for me."

"Thanks" Pete replied, "it's early days, but it's a good start I think."

"I am making a cooked breakfast at 8.30 if you want to join us" Stella told him.

He checked his watch; it was ten past 7.

"Yes, lovely," he said, "I can get a good bit more done by then, see you shortly."

He watched Stella head down the hill, she must be going for a morning walk. He stood and watched her until she was out of view and then shook himself out of his daydream and continued painting. He could lose himself in his painting, lose all sense of time so when Stella shouted that breakfast was ready, he couldn't believe it, hadn't he just watched her walk down the hill?

He put his brush down, it would be ok there for a little while, and he went to wash his paint covered hands before tucking into to bacon, fried eggs and toast. He could smell it as he walked back into the house and he was suddenly looking forward to hot food. At home he always ate cereal in the morning, he had learned to cook after Gill died but he never felt like it in the morning. He did make a mean omelette though and often had one with various fillings for his lunch.

"Morning ladies" he smiled as he sat down opposite Jayne "late night was it?"

"Morning Pete" replied Jayne "yes, it was a bit, I didn't disturb you did I, I was a little tipsy."

"Not at all" replied Pete "you look different this morning, more relaxed, this break must have done you good."

Jayne looked quite taken aback by Pete's comments, she did feel more relaxed but was it really that noticeable?

"Sorry" continued Pete "I didn't mean to put my size ten boot in it, it's just nice to see you looking less tense and when you get to my age somehow the polite filter doesn't engage like it used to. I seem to just say what I am thinking."

"That's OK" replied Jayne "you just caught me off guard. I am more relaxed and mainly thanks to our wonderful host, she helped me put a few things into perspective last night."

"You sound just like my mum, Pete" Stella joined in "as she has got older she just doesn't seem to care what she says" Stella laughed "not that she's rude particularly, just a little too honest sometimes. Anyway, Jayne, I agree that you look much less tense and much happier. Ready to go home now?"

"I am, I'll have a last walk along the sea and then head off just before midday."

"Well, it's been nice to meet you Jayne," said Pete "if you ladies will excuse me I am off back to my easel and my paints" Pete wasn't interested enough to find out what Jayne had on her mind but it was nice to see her lighten up.

He took a last swig of tea and pottered off into the garden leaving the ladies to chat over their breakfast.

He spent hours painting his sunrise, he had waved Jayne off at midday and eventually mid-afternoon was happy enough to put it away for the day and go for a walk. He would scope out the harbour for his next painting and find a café to enjoy a coffee and a doughnut. He had a thing for doughnuts, any type, ring ones, jam ones, custard ones, apple ones, any doughnut. He loved the feeling of the sugar round his mouth for hours afterwards, there always seemed to be a bit left.

He tidied all his painting equipment up into the barn and left his painting on the easel to dry. He then grabbed his jacket and set off down the hill, thinking he might have to get a taxi back up.

Jayne

Jayne was shocked at Pete's observation at breakfast, did she really look that different? Her few days here had been fabulous. It was definitely the best thing she could have done and having Stella there to talk to had been an added bonus. She did feel amazing from eating some good food and doing a lot of exercise along with the fresh sea air and some good company.

Jayne walked down the hill for her last walk by the sea before she drove home. She had decided that she would call John after she set off, she didn't want anything to spoil her last morning in this glorious place. She was feeling pretty good about going home though, she had missed John and although she knew things wouldn't change overnight, she did feel she was revitalised enough to deal with her life. She would make the small changes she decided with Stella and would do all she could to control herself when she wanted to change John.

She walked briskly with the wind in her face to start with until she came to the little beach hut café she had stopped at most days. She got her coffee to go today so she could walk back and buy John some Cornish cookies in the village, he did enjoy a good chocolate cookie. He had put on weight since he had been in the wheelchair, but he carried it well and it was nice to see him enjoy his food. It was the one thing that he did still enjoy, she was going to have to be careful with her weight when she got home.

She had definitely lost a couple of pounds, even over these few short days away. With all the walking she had done her trousers didn't cling quite so much and that was motivating her to want to keep the exercise up. As well as her Pilates class that she would book when she got back she also determined to walk a bit more. She planned to park her car further away from the office, that would give her another mile each day to walk unless it was raining of course.

She walked back up that killer hill in one sprint and was only slightly out of breath when she got to the top. She did stop to look at that view again, she was going to miss that, but she had a lovely garden at home to admire from her window. She walked past Pete on her way and admired his sunrise, he had talent.

She went to find Stella for one last coffee before she left, she found her tidying the sitting room.

"Hey" Jayne greeted her "I have made a couple of other decisions."

"Hey to you too, good for you, do you want to share?" Stella asked.

"Absolutely, so firstly I'd like to book myself back in here in 6 weeks' time. It has been so beneficial that I would like to become a regular, just a night or two but it can be me time."

"Fantastic" Stella was really pleased, "I think that's a great idea, and the other decision?"

"I am going to have an honest conversation with John, I am going to tell him how I am feeling and what I need whilst being careful not to sound like I am blaming him for anything. I have been thinking it through and I don't want to lie to him, so I will start with small conversations like the needing a cleaner and why I need one and about the exercise class. I could lie and say I have late meetings but that's not going to help our relationship. So, what do you think?"

"I think that is really sensible, treat him like an adult and like your husband, otherwise all you are doing is turning your relationship into a carer/patient one and that's not what you want. It's not going to be easy and prepare yourself for what his response might be. Don't get defensive, really listen to him and address any concerns together." Stella wanted Jayne to approach this with caution, after all these years it will be a big change for John, and it was also going to be a surprise when she talked to him.

"Thank you" replied Jayne "yes, I know I can be a bit like a bull in a china shop. When I get an idea in my head, I just want to get on with it, but I know I need to take it slow. Well, wish me luck."

"I do, I really wish you lots of luck," Stella said with feeling "you can tell me how it is going when you come back in 6 weeks' time."

They agreed which week that was and booked in. Jayne was happy to have it in the diary; it gave her something to look forward to. She went and collected her luggage from her room then gave Stella a big hug before setting off on her journey home. She had lots to think about on the journey and her first call was to ring John and tell him she was on her way.

"Hi Honey," she said cheerfully when he answered his phone "I'm on my way home, should be back by half three, I have some chocolate cookies for you."

"Lovely" he replied, "I have missed you, look forward to seeing you soon, drive carefully."

She was thrilled that he had missed her, maybe things would be alright with her life after all.

Stella

Stella waved Jayne off, she was so pleased that Jayne's break had resulted in good things, well, a good plan anyway. She was sure this wasn't going to be easy for Jayne, she imagined that Jayne probably tried to be the boss at home like she was at work. She understood that it was sometimes hard to change the focus from work to home. It had worked in Stella's life as Stuart was also in business and so they called each other out when they were too corporate at home. They had some huge rows over the years but always made up before they went to bed. Most of the time they rubbed along easily enjoying their relationship.

Jayne had been dealing with John's health issues for most of ten years, she had found a way to deal with all of her stresses and now she was going to change all that. Stella really wished her the best of luck and hoped that when she saw her again there was some kind of successful change. We will soon see, she thought.

Anyway, things to do. She saw Pete go off out for a walk so she reckoned she had a couple of hours to do some admin. She sat at her laptop and started with her accounts. Her website was set up so that her customers paid online for their bookings, she didn't want to have to deal with cash. They were instructed to pay 48 hours before arriving; so far so good. She checked that her books balanced. She had a meeting with her accountant each quarter where they made sure she was doing everything she should particularly around HMRC, taxes were just a mine-field.

Since Philip had corrected her website, she had taken quite a lot of bookings, every day she was seeing bookings pop up in her calendar. Now she would send each of them an e-mail as although the website did all the work, she always liked to add that personal touch. When she went in to update the calendar, she was thrilled to see that July was fully booked and in August she only had a few nights available. In the summer most of the bookings were for a week at a time. She suspected that in the high season she would be more of a B&B than a retreat but that was fine, probably easier in fact.

There was a group booking for a week in June, one person had booked all 5 rooms, she would need to find out more about that. She wrote an e-mail introducing herself and asking about the group and what plans they had for the week. She was very friendly in her contact and offered to arrange whatever they wanted.

Easter was another busy weekend, but two rooms were taken by her good friends Kirsty and Gail. She was looking forward to seeing them, it had been January the last time she had seen them. It was Easter next weekend, but she had a few empty days between Pete leaving on Monday and her first guests arriving on Thursday. That gave her plenty of time to get ready for a busy weekend.

After seeing all the bookings for the summer, she went back to her accounts to see if she could afford some additional staff. She needed a cleaner, that was the bit she didn't like doing. She would have a think about that over the weekend and maybe talk it through with her mum.

She heard Marie arrive but left her to it while she finished sending e-mails to all of her new customers. She finished up and felt very happy with how things were going. She went downstairs and treated herself to a glass of rosé. She and Marie chatted,

Marie was in good spirits and then she went to lay the table. Just her and Pete tonight, and she bought two fillet steaks when she walked past the butcher this morning and she had also bought some beer. She thought Pete was very much a steak and beer man and was sure he would enjoy his dinner tonight.

CHAPTER 33

Pete

Pete was relieved when he arrived for dinner to find steak, chunky chips and beer put in front of him. He had been slightly worried that it would be another healthy meal like last night, not that the food hadn't been good, it was just a little light for him.

"So, have you had a good day Pete?" asked Stella.

"I have, thank you" Pete replied, tucking into his chips.

"What did you get up to?" Stella pushed. She had discovered that Pete was a very quiet man and wasn't one to natter for the sake of it.

"Mainly painting" he replied, "I am quite pleased with it actually." His face lit up at the thought of his sunrise.

"How do you know what shades and shadows to paint?" Stella asked, realising he had such a passion for painting, that was going to be the subject to get him to open up a little.

In fact, he launched into a full explanation of how he had learned by making lots of mistakes and doing lots of bad paintings for years. Then eventually he had joined an art class where he learned so much, he couldn't believe how simple it could be once you understood about light and different style of brushes and other such stuff.

Pete recognised that he was a shy person and he often struggled to make general conversation with people, that's why painting suited him so much. He could do it alone and not have to enter into any irrelevant chat. He did enjoy talking about art though and so when Stella asked about techniques, he was happy to chat for ages answering her questions.

"I'm sorry," he said after a while "am I boring you? I get so carried away when talking about my painting."

"Not at all" said Stella "it's really interesting, I have never been very arty. I love looking at paintings, but I wouldn't know a good one from a bad one, I just know what I like."

"But that's the great thing about art" Pete replied "it should always be about what you like. Who cares if it's technically brilliant or some abstract award-winning art, it has to suit you. I don't care what anyone else thinks about my paintings, I paint what I like, and if someone else likes them too, then that's a bonus."

"What a great attitude to have," Stella smiled, she liked Pete "my mum's quite creative, she makes jewellery, just for herself and her friends; it's quite flamboyant some of it but it suits her."

"Does she?" asked Pete "that sounds interesting"

"She is staying for the weekend, she arrives tomorrow. We'll see what creation she will be adorned with at dinner tomorrow evening."

"I can't wait" laughed Pete. He enjoyed his dinner with Stella, she had a sense about her. She quickly learned what made him comfortable, how to have easy conversation and when not to push things. He had been impressed with the impact she made on Jayne; she was a different person when she left.

CHAPTER 34

Mum (aka Margaret)

Margaret was ready to go, she had packed last night, she had just eaten toast and jam for breakfast and now she was twitching the curtains waiting for her cab to arrive. She had a booked a first-class ticket on South Western trains and booked the cab to pick her up at 7 am. It was 6.53 and she was restless, coat on, bag over her arm, wheelie case by the front door, keys in her hand.

She was a seasoned traveller but for some reason, even though she had left plenty of time, she was always slightly anxious at this stage. Would the cab arrive on time, would they get stuck in traffic on the way to the station etc. Once she was on the train, she would be fine.

Ah, here he was. It was Dave, excellent, she liked Dave, he was nice and chatty and drove at a good pace. Mark was the one she didn't like; he drove like he was 100 years old; she didn't know how he got anywhere on time he was so slow. She used the same taxi firm all the time and now knew some of the regular drivers.

She opened the door before he rang the bell.

"Morning Dave, nice to see you, would you just grab the case please?"

"No problem Margaret" he replied, "Bournemouth station, is that right?"

"Yes, I am off to see my daughter in Cornwall, she has a new hotel there, it's just opened. I'm really looking forward to seeing it now it's up and running."

Dave loaded the case and helped Margaret into the back seat, not that she needed help. At 75 she was still fit and healthy and feeling good. She had lots of friends and spent her life doing lots of interesting things, keeping active and volunteering at the local food bank. She always felt grateful for her life even though it hadn't all been easy, she was financially secure and in good health, what more could you ask for?

There was no traffic and so she was at the station in plenty of time. She went and grabbed a coffee and a chocolate bar from the station kiosk. It was most of 5 hours on the train and so she had packed a good book, some sandwiches and some fruit in her bag. The train was on time and as she decided that she could afford the first-class ticket, she benefited from having an allocated seat. She made herself comfortable and sipped her coffee watching the countryside speed by.

She thought about her two daughters, Stella and Judith, so different. Stella had always been the one that she thought would end up running something, even when she was little, she was always the organiser. When she played in the Wendy house that their dad built for them Stella would be leaving her friend Colin cooking whilst she went off to work. Margaret smiled at the image; it was no surprise that Stella had focussed on her career and not had children. Judith was the academic of the family, she loved learning, spent a lot of time in her bedroom alone. She went to university where she studied chemistry, then on to get her PhD. She ended up working in pharmaceuticals before meeting Brad at a convention in New York. Now she was married to Brad with two gorgeous boys and living in the Big Apple.

They weren't close, her two girls but they got on fine, they were so different. She knew they kept in touch and she was looking forward to them all getting together later in the year.

Margaret still missed their dad, Gerald. He died 7 years ago now and he had been a fabulous husband and father. Their early life was hard; they both came from relatively poor backgrounds and hadn't done well at school. When they first married, they lived in two rooms rented above the shop that Margaret worked in, it was tiny and cold. Gerald worked at the docks and accepted all the overtime he could in order to save up for a deposit on a flat. They were determined to own their own home before they had a family and they did. It was just a small flat, but it was on the ground floor which meant it came with a small patch of garden.

Over the years they were frugal but provided their daughters with everything they needed. Gerald did really well at the docks and eventually became the Operations Director. This meant that Margaret could become a full-time mum for a while until the girls were at secondary school when she went back to work part time in the fashion section of the town's department store.

Anyway, she was on her way to see her eldest daughter and she was looking forward to it. She had visited a few times since Stella bought Hilltop but knew that it would have changed a lot since the last time. She was proud that Stella really did own her own business and was running her own retreat. After she sampled it Margaret was sure she would be able to push a few clients her way, she had lots of friends that could afford a nice break away by the sea.

She read her book the rest of the way interspersed with lifting her head to look at the scenery and changing trains which she had to do twice. She was good at trains, so she wasn't fazed by the changes, she had looked it all up beforehand and Stella was picking her up at Truro.

As the train pulled into Truro station Margaret was, as usual, ready to disembark. She double checked she had everything and then got off the train and into the waiting arms of her daughter.

"Hi Mum, you look great, how was the journey?" Stella hugged her mum hard.

"Hi honey" she laughed, "let me breathe, the journey was fine, now let me look at you" she pulled away and took a step back to look at her with pride "you look amazing, this new life must agree with you, you even have a bit of colour."

They chatted continuously on the 25-minute drive back to Hilltop filling each other in on their news.

Stella

After her early morning walk, Stella set about making sure the room was ready for her mum and that the house was looking immaculate. Her mum didn't judge other people, but she did like things to be clean and tidy and Stella wanted her mum to see how well she was doing in her new venture.

Pete was up and so the two of them enjoyed an early breakfast of bacon rolls, yoghurts and coffee. It was a quiet breakfast both of them in their own worlds thinking about their day. Stella was looking forward to seeing her mum and Pete was thinking about tinkering with his sunrise painting. Stella was grateful for the peace this morning, some days it was just nice for things to be relaxed and quiet.

Pete broke the silence "What time are you expecting your mother today?" he asked.

"Huh" Stella broke from her thoughts "Oh, her train is due in at 1.20 at Truro which is about 25-minute drive. It will be nice to see her."

"I look forward to meeting her," Pete said, "she sounds quite a character."

"She is" Stella replied cheerfully "she is a great mum and since my dad died, she's not stopped, she travels, she is a member of all sorts of clubs, she has more friends than I do and she looks amazing. What are you going to paint today?"

"I think I will tweak the sunrise and then later I'll start to think about the harbour view I'd like to paint. I might walk down there later this afternoon if the weather stays good."

"It's supposed to be dry all weekend, fingers crossed" Stella said as she started to clear up the breakfast plates. Pete thanked her for breakfast then he wandered off to the barn to play with his paints.

Stella tidied up the dining room and kitchen, she didn't want to get into trouble with Marie for leaving things in a mess. Then she went and took a shower and made herself look nice to meet her mum. She attended to some e-mail replies she had received from her proactive mails yesterday; everyone was pleased with her introduction, that was proving to be a good strategy.

The lady who booked all the rooms for a week in June had replied as well; it was a small group of young ladies on a Hen do. Fiona, the lady who was organising the trip had listed the sort of things they would like to do whilst they were there, if possible, including yoga, meditation, something on the water/beach and anything to do with chocolate and prosecco.

Stella smiled; she would enjoy arranging a few events for the ladies as it sounded like it would be a fun week. She just hoped they wouldn't be too unruly. She replied saying that she would look into what was available and would get back in touch nearer the time to finalise things.

She had received payment from her two bookings at Easter, Gregory Smythe, who seemed to promote himself as some kind of wellness guru, and Donna and Kevin Young. Stella knew Donna once many years ago, she was a graphic designer and found out about Hilltop on Facebook. She booked herself and her husband in for two nights. It would be nice to catch up with Donna; it was years since she had heard from her.

Stella sent a WhatsApp to Kirsty and Gail, her two friends, to check what time they were arriving on Good Friday and to see if they were driving or training. She wanted to make it a special weekend for them, they had been such great friends over the years particularly when Stuart had been ill and then passed away. Stella, Kirsty and Gail had all had their own dramas over the years, but they had always been there for each other, it was almost like they took it turns to have some disaster or other to deal with.

Admin all done, Stella sat down for a bowl of soup and a slice of doorstep crusty bread freshly made and delivered from the bakers that morning. She knew her mum would eat on the train, probably a homemade sandwich wrapped in one of her many types of sandwich bag.

She checked on Pete as she was leaving, he was in his element fine tuning his sunrise, she told him she would be back later and to help himself to anything he needed. She suspected, when she got back with her mum he would still be exactly where he was now.

It was a good journey to Truro, and she had to wait a while for the train to arrive. She sat in her car listening to the radio and singing along to the tunes. The train was on time and she was there waiting on the platform when her mum got off.

She hugged her mum hard, gosh it was good to see her, and she looked great. She grabbed her mum's case and led her to the car, they chatted non-stop on the drive back to Hilltop. Stella told her all about her guests, about Lucy and Grace and how much she had enjoyed their company. How she thought one day Lucy would be a big famous Hollywood movie Director and about Grace's disastrous love life. She told her about Jayne and how she thought she may have been able to help her resolve some of the conflict going on inside herself and about Pete the quiet painter who she thought had some grief still to work through.

She also told her mum about Rebecca, the child that had gone missing almost 50 years ago and the rumours of the ghost at Hilltop, which is said to be the distraught mother that had lost her child.

"How dreadful," her mum exclaimed "I think I would haunt the place if I lost my daughter, I just can't imagine something happening to you or your sister. The ghost must be waiting for her Rebecca to return one day."

Stella laughed "There is no ghost mum, it's just stories the locals made up. It's probably why I got such a good deal on buying it."

A few minutes later they pulled into the drive.

"Oh, your garden is looking great," said Margaret "you have done a super job for someone that knows nothing about gardening."

"I have had to learn all sorts of things to run this place, but I'd love for you to give me some advice on what else needs doing in the garden. Come and meet Pete, I'm sure he'll still be in the barn."

Sure enough, Pete was still ensconced in his paints, he had paint all over his hands and face and looked like a guilty child when he looked up to see Stella and Margaret walk in.

"Hi Pete, this is Margaret, my mum, we thought we'd just say hello, but it looks like you are busy with your paints there," said Stella.

"Ah, yes, well I kinda got caught up with it and lost all track of time." Pete put his hand out to shake Margaret's hand and then pulled it away quickly when he realised how mucky he was "nice to meet you" he said instead.

"We are going to put the kettle on if you would like to join us for tea?" Stella asked.

"Hum, yes maybe" Pete mumbled looking back at his painting.

Stella showed her mum into the house and took up to her room to dump her luggage "I am not sure we'll see Pete for tea, he does seem to get caught up with his art and loses all track of time. Make yourself comfortable, unpack your stuff and I'll be in the sitting room with a pot of tea and some fresh pastries when you are ready."

Pete

Pete realised he must have looked like an idiot after Stella and her mum had come to say hello. Here he was covered in paint, like a child, and he had just mumbled his way through hellos and turned back to his painting. Some first impression he must have made.

The truth was, that when Margaret had appeared in the doorway, he had felt something that he hadn't felt in a long, long time, not since he had first set eyes on Gill all those years ago. He had never expected to feel that way ever again and so it had caught him by surprise when his tummy had done cartwheels and his heart had almost exploded out of his chest. He was 69 for goodness sake, what was going on?

What should he do now? Should he tidy himself up and join them for tea? He could try and set a new first impression. Or should he just hide here in the barn and avoid her until he left on Monday? He couldn't avoid her all weekend, don't be stupid.

He picked up his mobile and dialled Samuel.

"Hey dad" Samuel answered cheerfully "how are you, how's the retreat and the painting going?"

"Oh good, good, thanks Son, um......"

"What is it dad, is everything ok?"

"Yes, well I've got a bit of a problem" Pete whispered into the phone "I don't know what to do."

"Why are you whispering, what is it? What's happened?" Pete could hear the panic in his son's voice, he hadn't meant to worry him."

"Oh, it's nothing really, no, don't you worry son, I'll sort myself out," Pete said.

"No, now you have to tell me dad or I'll be worrying all weekend, what is it?"

Pete sighed, he wished he hadn't called Samuel but now he had he said: "I think I've just fallen in love, I have made a terrible first impression, I'm hiding in the barn covered in paint, god knows what Stella and her mum think of my behaviour and I don't know what to do next."

Samuel laughed loudly in his dads' ear "Oh dad, I thought something bad had happened but that's fantastic, who is she this lady you are in love with?"

"Well, its Stella's mum, the lady that owns the retreat, it's her mum Margaret. I have only said hello, but my body is in meltdown, just like when I met your mum. It's just that I was rather rude when she came to say hello."

"Right," said Samuel, trying not to keep laughing, "here's the plan. Go and tidy yourself up, clean all the paint off then you can go and meet her again. Apologise for being rude, tell her you were caught up in your painting and you'd like to start over."

"Yes, right, good plan, thanks Son, gotta go" Pete hung up.

He quickly tidied the barn then marched into the house and up to his room before he could change his mind. He showered and put on his smart trousers and a nice casual shirt, he checked himself in the mirror, thought he'd do and took a big breath before walking down to the sitting area.

"Hi," he said, "I'm sorry for being rude before in the barn, I was caught up in my painting" he paused in the doorway.

Margaret smiled back at him "That's OK Pete, Stella said you were very focussed when you were painting, come in and join us."

Pete smiled thankfully at Stella and sat down in an armchair with a swarm of butterflies in his tummy.

Margaret

Margaret had tried not to laugh at Pete when Stella introduced her, he looked like a child with paint everywhere, hands, face, everywhere. He obviously loved his art and, at the very brief glimpse she got, his sunrise looked pretty good. He had been completely preoccupied with it and she pulled Stella away as she felt like they were intruding on his personal space. She thought he was a fine-looking man under all that paint but perhaps a little aloof. She hoped he would join them for coffee.

When Stella took her into the house, she was amazed at how different it looked to the last time she saw it. It was really classy, and it felt very peaceful, an overwhelming atmosphere of calmness, she thought. She loved her room and after unpacking, she spent a few moments sitting in the chair admiring the view. She was so proud of Stella and how she had dealt with Stuart's sudden death and come out the other side a stronger person now with her own business. She just knew it would be a success.

She met Stella in the sitting room but before they poured the tea, they went for a quick walk in the garden. Margaret loved gardening and so gave Stella some pointers as to the best things to plant for the summer colour. When they got to the point that looked over the pathway, where Pete had set up to paint his sunrise earlier, Stella stopped and said:

"This is around the spot that poor Rebecca went missing, she had been playing here when her mum went in to answer the telephone. The story goes that when she came back out Rebecca had just disappeared. I was thinking of planting something here as a memorial, what do you think would be suitable?"

"What about an aster?" Margaret suggested "its Greek for "Star" and they are known to attract butterflies, they come in all sorts of colours."

"Sounds perfect, I'll pop out to the garden centre at some stage and get some, thank you. Now let's go and have a cuppa."

Margaret thought it was a lovely idea to plant flowers in memory of that young girl, she had felt a shiver when she stood on that spot, just thinking about such a sad story. She was looking forward to a nice cup of tea though and the pastry. She had quite a sweet tooth and loved pastries and cakes, but she tried not to eat too many as she was determined not to get fat.

Stella poured tea and they sat happily drinking, munching and chatting when a shadow appeared in the doorway. Pete was looking shifty. Margaret and Stella looked up as he started to apologise for his behaviour earlier. Margaret caught Stella's eye then quickly looked away, so she didn't giggle. Bless him, he thought he'd been rude when she had just thought he was preoccupied. She accepted his explanation and invited him in to join them.

It seemed that Pete had a sweet tooth as he ate his way through two Danish pastries whilst he sat listening to Margaret and Stella talking. He obviously liked his food, Margaret thought; she could see his belly starting to hang over his belt. It wasn't as obvious when he was standing as he was a tall, stocky man and carried the weight easily. She admired his looks now that he was cleaned up and she could see his features. He was a very smiley man but very quiet, she tried to involve him in the conversation.

"What do you think of Hilltop Pete?" she asked him.

"It's perfect," he said, "the views are spectacular, and it just feels so calm here, it's the perfect place to paint."

"I agree, calm is how I felt when I arrived here today, she has done a great job, my Stella, hasn't she" Margaret put her hand on Stella's knee "not that I am biased at all you know."

"Thanks Mum" Stella blushed "now, would you two be OK if I go and see if Marie needs any help in the kitchen and everything is on track for dinner at 7.30?"

"Of course, darling, you go and do what you need to, Pete and I will be just fine here won't we Pete?"

"Um, yes, of course," Pete looked nervous about being left alone with Margaret, but she was very good at getting the quietest of people to chat to her. Stella left them with a fresh pot of tea and went to get the dining room ready and chat to Marie.

Margaret was grateful that Stella had left them alone, she thought she might really like Pete, and she wanted to get to know him a bit better. She wondered what be the best subject to talk about, art, maybe, as a starting point.

She was right, as Stella had discovered Pete loved talking about art and his painting and, once Margaret asked how he got started painting, he was off. He talked for ages before he took a breath and smiled at her, he asked her;

"Stella tells me you make jewellery, what sort of stuff do you make?"

Now it was Margaret's turn, she told him that she had always loved shiny stuff and when she was first married, she couldn't afford nice jewellery, so she bought a kit and it all started from there.

"We were very poor when we were young and so we had to find ways to make do, Gerald would make beer from a kit and I would make bracelets from beads, we had some fun. I made jewellery with the girls when they were growing up and then stopped for many years especially when we could afford to buy better stuff. When Gerald died, I picked it up again as something to do, I have even sold a few bits at craft fairs and on e-bay."

"Have you?" asked Pete, "have you got some I can see?"

"Well, I made this bracelet" she shook her arm so that the bracelet showed itself from under her sleeve "and I have a stunning necklace I will wear to dinner tonight."

Pete stood up and came over and sat in the chair that Stella had vacated next to Margaret, she held out her arm for him to see the bracelet. It was a simple beaded band, but the beads caught the sunlight and it was sparkling. She jumped slightly at his gentle touch on her arm, then smiled as their eyes met, yes, she definitely wanted to get to know Pete better.

Pete

Pete loved Margaret's bracelet and he went to have a closer look. When he brushed against her skin, he got an electric shock, he felt her twitch slightly and when he looked up her eyes met his and they both smiled. Oh boy, he thought. I am so out of practice at this, don't make a fool of yourself.

He enjoyed listening to her talk about her jewellery making and about her early beginnings back in her younger days. A thought came to him and he said

"Would you like to join me in a stroll down to the harbour? I was going to scope out what to paint and we still have a while until dinner?" please say yes, please say yes he was thinking.

"I'd love to Pete, I can work off that pastry I've eaten, let me just change my shoes and let Stella know."

Pete was grinning, he couldn't stop it, he watched her disappear out of the room to get herself ready and just sat grinning like a Cheshire cat. He had to try hard to be serious when Stella popped in to say

"You look happy Pete" Stella had caught sight of the grin and grinned herself, it was infectious

"mum says you two are going for a walk, just to remind you dinner is at 7.30, lamb chops tonight. Have a good walk."

"Thanks Stella, we'll be back in plenty of time, I'll look after your mum."

Stella laughed "I'm more worried about you Pete, look after yourself, she might lead you astray."

"Who might?" Margaret asked walking back into the room "you cheeky thing, come on Pete, let's get out of here."

Stella waved them off and Pete could see her out of the corner of his eye as they walked down the path, he knew she hadn't gone back in until they were out of sight. He turned his attention back to Margaret and how regal she was. She was trim and smart, "well turned out," his Gill would have said. He thought he would need to neaten himself up a bit if he wanted to meet her standards. He hadn't worried too much over the last few years. He hadn't let himself go or anything, but he didn't have a woman's eye to help him look his best. Gill had always made sure he was dressed just right for any occasion. He had been OK at work, standard suit with a white shirt served him well and out of work casual was OK too, jeans and a polo shirt was his go to outfit which he felt was almost always appropriate. Any other events he struggled with which is why he sometimes just didn't go.

"A penny for them?" Margaret nudged him.

"Oh, sorry, miles away" Pete replied, "I was just looking at the harbour down there and wondering where the best view of it will be to paint it."

He could tell Margaret didn't believe him, but she went with it.

"Well, are you thinking of doing a view of the whole harbour, in which case you need to be higher up, or a view of a portion or even just one boat, in which case we need to be down there?"

"Let's go and have a look down there by the boatshed" Pete said, he wondered if they would be allowed on the piers where the boats were moored. He was thinking he would do a close up of one boat with the rest of the harbour in the background. He shared his thought with Margaret who agreed it sounded like a great idea.

"Let's go and ask if we can access the moorings then" she was rushing ahead to the boat shed before he had a chance to try and hold her back.

"Excuse me," Margaret said loudly to the young man working in the shed "are you the person to talk to about accessing the piers, is that even the right word?"

Pete had caught up with her now and was grabbing her arm.

"Let's not bother the chap, he's busy working" Pete never wanted to be any trouble, he would have thought about it much more before taking any action.

"No trouble," said the young man "I'm Jason, I run the boatyard, what is it you want?"

"Pete here, would like to paint the harbour but would really like to get in close to the boats, is that possible?" Margaret asked.

"I don't see why not." smiled Jason "Evening is the best time as most of the boats are moored up and you wouldn't get in people's way. When were you thinking of doing it?"

"Tomorrow, if that is ok with you, I can do tomorrow evening, this sort of time perhaps?" Pete said.

"That's settled then, thank you, Jason. See that was easy," she whispered to Pete.

Pete shook Jason's hand and then led Margaret away "You are going to be bad for me, or maybe good for me!" Pete laughed at himself "let's grab a takeaway coffee and sit on the harbour wall for a while."

"You romantic you" Margaret tucked her arm in his and they ambled along to the coffee shop and with Styrofoam cups in hand, they sat on the wall chatting about their lives, their families, their likes and dislikes until Margaret's phone buzzed.

"Oh My, Pete" Margaret exclaimed "do you know what time it is? It's gone 7, we better get back or I'll be in trouble with my daughter.

"Goodness let's grab a taxi; I'll be damned if I am rushing up that hill."

They piled into a taxi, laughing, and were back at Hilltop in a few short minutes where, after a tongue in cheek dressing down from Stella, they both went and tidied themselves for dinner.

CHAPTER 35

Stella

S tella had noticed that Pete had developed a soft spot for her mum, which was why she left them alone to get to know each other. Her mum could do with some male company and Pete would definitely have an adventure with her mum. She wasn't surprised when they decided to go out for a walk together although she was surprised to find that it was Pete that had instigated it, maybe he was braver than she thought.

She busied herself helping Marie with dinner and laying the table then went and did some admin before dinner was ready. There was so much admin to do, but she did her best to keep on top of it. Whilst she was at her laptop, she looked up the asters her mum had mentioned, oh yes, they were pretty. The thought of Rebecca led her to do a little more research on the Bartley family.

It seems that Arthur Bartley was born at Hilltop and grew up to run a very successful building firm that he started in 1942; he was only 20 when he started it. He had married Florence in 1941 and their two children were born in quick succession, Jennifer in 1941 and Robert in 1942. Robert had joined his dad in the building firm and kept it running. The firm was still trading now.

Stella googled Bartley builders and found it on the internet. There was a brief description of it being a family firm and is now run by Simon and Martin Bartley. They must be Robert's children, Stella thought.

She found the marriage of Jennifer to Christopher Pine in 1961, he was the Manager of the local department store. She also found the records of the two children Geoffrey born in 1962 and Rebecca born in 1965

Arthur died at age 52 from a sudden heart attack, Stella found a news article about it online and looked at the pictures of the funeral. It was a massive turnout; he was a very popular local figure. The article also mentioned the devastation of the family regarding the disappearance of Arthur's granddaughter Rebecca in 1969.

Stella was confused at why Rebecca went missing from Hilltop as Jennifer and Christopher didn't live there at the time, they had their own cottage in the village. She delved a little further and found some of the articles written about the disappearance. It seems that Jennifer had taken to spending warm days up at her parents' house as they had such a lovely garden, whereas her cottage had a tiny courtyard. On the day of the disappearance Florence had been helping Arthur with some paperwork down at the building yard and Jennifer and the children were alone at Hilltop.

A few months after the disappearance, Jennifer and Christopher moved into the annexe at Hilltop presumably so that Florence could help look after Geoffrey. Stella imagined Jennifer was struggling to deal with at all. Arthur died 5 years, later leaving Florence as the owner of Hilltop. It seemed that Jennifer never moved back to the cottage, but that Christopher shared his time between the cottage and Hilltop. Stella would love to know more, she imagined they all dealt with it in very different ways.

Christopher died in 2008, he was 76 and Jennifer died only a few months later. She was only 68, they said she died of a broken heart. It seemed, for all their troubles, Christopher was her lifeline and when he died, she lost the will to live. Geoffrey doesn't seem to have factored much in their lives after he left Hilltop to move to London in his late teens.

Stella had bought the house from Florence Bartley, but she only ever dealt with the Estate agent and the solicitor. The house stood empty for some time before she took ownership of it and she knew nothing about its history. Stella closed her laptop down feeling she knew a little bit more about the Bartley family now.

She walked downstairs at 7 o clock to find Marie in a mild panic.

"Where is everyone?" she asked, "Dinners almost ready and there is no-one here. Usually I pop out to see people enjoying a glass of wine but it's all quiet."

"Don't worry Marie, I'm sure they'll be here in time" Stella wasn't sure at all, Pete was always losing track of time. She texted her mum and got an "on our way" text back.

Ten minutes later she heard lots of laughter as her mum and Pete waved the taxi off and rushed into the hallway.

"So sorry," Mum said, "we lost all track of time, won't be a minute."

They both ran up the stairs and returned a few minutes later looking smart and composed.

Stella couldn't be cross with them, they looked like two love struck teenagers and they managed to get to the table just about before Marie dished up. They had obviously loved their walk and time together. They told Stella about meeting Jason and that Pete would go back down there at about 4 pm tomorrow afternoon to paint a picture of the harbour.

"Would you prefer that I did a lunchtime roast tomorrow then

Pete? "Stella asked, "That way you won't have to worry about getting back in time tomorrow evening, you can stay and paint to your heart's content."

Pete looked up from his food "Would that be ok, that would be great?"

"That's fine, I'll do lunch for 1 o clock tomorrow," Stella said, "Mum can give me a hand seeing as Marie doesn't work Sundays, and we can have a good natter whilst we are cooking?"

"Perfect," said her mum. Then she raised her glass and said: "Cheers, here's to new friends."

CHAPTER 36

Margaret

Margaret admitted to herself she had enjoyed Pete's company yesterday and the three of them having dinner together just put the cherry on top. She didn't know what the future would hold but she was just happy to have some fun along the way. He was much more reserved than she was, but she spotted a spark of life hidden away there, she thought he was open to trying new things and he really was a gentleman.

She felt that spark again when she saw him at breakfast before he headed off to do some painting and she went to help Stella prepare a Sunday roast. She was ambushed when she walked into the kitchen, her daughter wanted to know everything.

"So, you saucy minx," Stella said to her "tell me all, what's happened between you and Pete then? Come on spill the beans."

Margaret laughed "just some harmless fun."

"Good for you mum, it's about time you had some male company, he seems really nice," Stella said.

"Actually Stel, I think I really like him. I know, I know, I've only just met him but there is a definite spark there, I'm pretty sure he feels it too. I think that's what made him a bit offish when I first met him in the barn yesterday."

"Really, love at first sight hey?"

"Well why not, I'm not bad for my age?" Margaret retorted.

"You look amazing mum; he'd be lucky to have you. I think you've found yourself a toy boy."

They chatted away while they chopped vegetables and got the beef joint ready to pop in the oven. Margaret made an apple and blackberry crumble for dessert.

"How's Grandma?" Stella asked, "I really must give her a call, I haven't spoken to her for a couple of weeks, it's been so busy here."

"Oh, same old, she's really lost it now, she doesn't always even remember me when I visit, she just wants to die."

"She's been saying that for 20 years since Grandad died!"

"I know, but it's really bad now. The carers are great at the home but it's not a nice place to be and I only stop for an hour now, I can't bear it any longer. You know Pete has the same issue, his mum is 94 and has turned into a miserable cow. Apparently, she used to be life and soul and now she is just unhappy. There should be a better way, don't go shoving me in a care home to waste away, will you?"

They moved on to more cheerful subjects and had a lovely few hours together before they called Pete for lunch. It was a sociable Sunday lunch with Pete opening up a bit more about his mum, his daughter and his son and his family.

Margaret liked Pete more and more as he opened up and was pleasantly shocked when she felt his foot find hers under the table. She didn't want to look at Stella or she would giggle and so she tried to keep up a sensible conversation. She could see Stella knew there was something going on and after dessert Stella suggested she and Pete take a coffee into the sitting room leaving her to clear up.

She spent a lovely hour chatting to Pete until he went to get his paints ready and he headed off down to the harbour. She would pop down there later on with a sandwich and a flask of coffee; in the meantime, she would spend some quality time with her daughter over another glass of wine.

Stella

Stella spent a wonderful day with her mum, it was great to see her looking so well, and so funny that she had hit it off with Pete. Her mum had just set off with a picnic to see Pete at the harbour and Stella was just about to sit and watch some trashy tv when her phone rang. Who would be calling on a Sunday evening?

"Hello, Hilltop" Stella answered.

"Ah, hello," a Scottish lady said, "I wondered if there was any chance you had a room free for a couple of nights from tomorrow."

"I do" Stella replied, "just one room, one person, would you like an evening meal?"

"Och, brilliant" the lady replied "yes one person and an evening meal would be perfect, thank you. My name is Lizzie McDonald, I'll be there tomorrow afternoon, I think the train gets to Truro at 3.30, I guess I'll get a cab from there?"

Stella took all her details and took payment and agreed to pick her up at Truro tomorrow, she was dropping her mum back to the station tomorrow anyway. She would have a bit of time to kill but she would do some shopping, maybe even buy the asters.

Well, that's a bit more business, thought Stella; never turn business away. She wondered what her new guest would be like. She went back to her trashy tv and dozed off on her sofa when she heard her mum and Pete get back from the harbour. She looked at her watch, it was 9.30, they must have run out of light ages ago.

She went to meet them in the barn where Pete showed them both the sunrise and the harbour so far.

"These are amazing Pete; even unfinished you can see how great the harbour view will be. Seriously would you come back one day and paint Hilltop for me, I'll pay you for it?"

Pete smiled with pride "I'll paint it for you for free if you put me up for free while I paint it."

"Deal," said Stella "cup of tea anyone?"

Stella made them all tea and a piece of hot toast each. She told them about her new guest arriving tomorrow and that she would drop mum off and collect her at Truro.

"What?" said Stella, as her mum and Pete looked at each other shiftily.

"Well, Pete's offered to drive me to the station tomorrow, we thought it would save you the journey."

"Oh, OK, well that fine, it will save me hanging around between trains, thanks Pete," said Stella. That was fine with her, she could tidy up and take her time getting things ready after Pete and her mum left in the morning.

Margaret

Margaret was packed and ready to head off as soon as they had eaten breakfast. She wandered down to join Stella and was pleased to find Pete already there tucking into a full English.

"I saw your ghost last night" she announced as she sat down and poured a coffee.

"There is no ghost mum, you must have had a dream" Stella sighed.

"What ghost?" asked Pete.

"Oh, don't you know there is a ghost here, I saw her at the edge of the garden as I was getting ready for bed last night. It was a definite ghostly shadow of a woman."

"Really? "asked Pete "is that where I was painting?"

"Yes, why?"

"Because I felt a definite chill a few times when I was painting the other day, it was like a cloud had passed over me," said Pete "who is the ghost then?"

"I'll tell you all about it in the car," said Margaret "it's quite a tearjerker."

Margaret enjoyed her breakfast and, after spending half an hour alone with Stella whilst Pete packed up the car, they set off and she waved to Stella for as long as she could still see her at the gate. She had enjoyed her weekend with her daughter, and found a man to boot, who knew?

She chattered away on the drive to the station; she told Pete all about the ghost she had seen and the sad story of Rebecca's disappearance. Then they talked about more cheerful things as she didn't want to leave on a sad note.

"So, Pete," Margaret said "would you like to meet up again sometime, I'd say yes if you asked me out for dinner"

Pete smiled, she wasn't shy at all and he loved that about her "Would you like to go out to dinner with me Margaret?"

"Yes Pete, I'd love to" they both laughed.

"Here's my number" Margaret showed him the piece of paper as she popped it in the glove box "you give me a call when you get home and can check your diary and we'll arrange a date."

"Will do," said Pete.

He pulled into the station and he got out of the car with her.

Before she left, they had a big embrace, her heart fluttered, and she hoped that he would call her.

CHAPTER 37

Lizzie

Lizzie dumped her bag on the sofa and walked to the fridge, she grabbed a Kit Kat, to hell with it, she grabbed the whole packet of Kit Kats and a can of diet coke. She plonked herself down next to her bag and snivelled which turned into crying which turned into full blown hysterics. She rummaged for the tissues in her bag, she had gone prepared today, she knew she would be upset.

She cried herself out and then she switched on the television. She found some comedy and sat and munched her way through 5 Kit Kats. She switched between laughing and crying some more before she found the energy to go and change out of her smart black dress. She picked up the high heels she had kicked off when she got in and went to find some comfy jogging bottoms to slob about in. She stopped as she passed the mirror and stared in horror at the mess she was. Her face was red and tear-stained, it was all blotchy and her eyes were wet, they wouldn't stop leaking.

She moved away from the mirror quickly and went and ran a bubble bath. She would soak in some Lavender and then would slob about for the evening before she pulled herself together to-morrow; she had things to deal with.

The bath helped soothe her somewhat and then she sat, and comfort ate all evening. She ordered and ate a large pepperoni pizza with garlic bread and coleslaw and downed a whole bottle of cava whilst binge watching Netflix; not that her mind was on it.

It had been a nice service, she thought, and a decent turnout. Everyone from the hamlet had turned up and quite a lot of people from the surrounding areas. Her mum had been a district nurse and so knew a lot of people here in the highlands. It was a large patch she had covered and she had only stopped working when she got ill two years ago. She had just celebrated her 80th birthday last month and after that, it was like she gave up. It was like; she aimed to get to 80, then all bets were off.

Lizzie was close to her mum and was devasted by her death. She moved back home last year when her mum needed taking care of and they enjoyed lots of quality time together reminiscing. Lizzie's dad left when Lizzie turned 18; she saw him a couple of times of year but as he now lived in London, it was a long way to go from Scotland. That made her and her mum even closer. Lizzie left school with a couple of A Levels and got herself an admin job at the local newspaper. She had worked there off and on for 35 years and was now the editor.

Lizzie had married Ben when she was 23 but after trying for many years to have children, the strain on the marriage was eventually too much and he left her, to breed like rabbits with Nancy. Good luck to them.

Anyway, back to grieving. Lizzie fell asleep on the sofa having worn herself out with her emotions and, when she woke in the middle of the night, she dragged herself off to bed.

When she woke in the morning, she was feeling puffy and drained, but she had a shower and made an effort to get dressed. She made herself egg on toast for breakfast, with lashings of butter and jam. She knew mum had a will stored in the top of her wardrobe, her mum had told her, but she hadn't been able to bring herself to look at it before now. She assumed everything had been left to her, not that she cared about the money but there wasn't anyone else.

She pulled the cardboard storage box down and opened it up, goodness there was loads of stuff in here, must be all old memorabilia that her mum had kept. She found the will easily enough; it was in a bright red envelope with "LAST WILL AND TESTAMENT" written on it. She opened it up and was glad to see it was typed and she didn't have to cope with seeing her mums handwriting; it did indeed leave everything to her. She put it to one side, she would go to the solicitors later to find out what to do about it.

She braced herself to look through the memorabilia, she knew it was going to bring out a full set of emotions from sadness to joy to laughter. She found one of her school reports, her baby teeth, a few special birthday cards, a keyring she had made at school, a bit of rubbish embroidery, and lots of other things she had completely forgotten about.

She pulled out a brown envelope with 'R' written on the front, it was a tatty envelope, must be very old. She tipped the contents onto the floor and her life changed forever.

CHAPTER 38

Stella

Stella waved her mum and Pete off, they made a handsome couple she thought, she hoped they would keep in touch. Pete lived less than an hour away from her mum so it would certainly be doable. She felt that the break had been good for both of them, it was great to see her mum flirting again and Pete seemed to have had a lovely time here at the seaside. She would contact him soon to see when he could come back and do her painting for her, it would be fab to have an original painting of Hilltop.

She turned and walked inside; she had a little bit of time now before she went and picked Lizzie up this afternoon. She popped her earphones in and set about stripping and making the beds, got the washing on, run the vacuum round and made sure everything was spic and span. When she was happy it all looked perfect, she made herself a light lunch and then set off. She wanted to go to the garden centre on the way to pick up some asters.

She pulled in at the garden centre; it was heaving. She found a parking space and got a trolley; you know one of those trolleys that had a mind of its own. It didn't like turning corners, in the end, she pulled it rather than pushed it, that seemed to work a bit better.

She found the asters, they were pretty, she chose 3 plants of pink and white, suitable for a little girl. She also bought a selection of other attractive plants for her borders. She knew very little about plants, but they looked nice. She also bought a few decorative garden stakes; a butterfly, a bee and a sunflower, they would brighten the borders up. She paid and loaded up the boot of her car leaving enough room for any luggage Lizzie McDonald might have.

She set off for Truro and arrived at the station with enough time to grab a coffee from the kiosk. She had made herself a little placard with "Lizzie McDonald" written on it, as she had no idea what Lizzie looked like and vice versa. She felt a bit self-conscious holding it as the train pulled in but better than them missing each other.

She was standing by the exit when a short plump lady stopped in front of her; all Stella noticed was pink! Lizzie was wearing a pink jacket and carrying a pink case "Hi there, I'm Lizzie, you must be Stella, pleased to meet you" she said in a broad Scottish accent.

"Hi Lizzie, pleased to meet you too, my car is just over here. Can I help with your bags?"

"Och, no, its fine lassie, lead the way."

They loaded her case and rucksack into the boot amongst the flowers and she held on to her rather large handbag, keeping it close to her.

"How was your journey?" asked Stella "long way from Scotland."

"Indeed" Lizzie answered "it was fine, I had some work to do on the way down and I managed to grab a wee nap as well. I've never been to Cornwall before so it will be nice to have a squint around, hopefully it will be worth the 9-hour trip."

"I'm sure it will, it's a wonderful area, everything is blooming now that its spring and the weather has been lovely, not that I can guarantee that for you."

"No, well that's disappointing" Lizzie laughed a deep hearty laugh "compared to the Highlands its positively balmy down here."

"Are you just on holiday here?" asked Stella.

"Yes and no" answered Lizzie "that's a little cryptic isn't it? I am combining a break with a bit of research."

"Oh" said Stella "what sort of research?"

"Well, I'm an editor at a local paper, back home and a story came to my attention that may or may not pan out and having never been down here I thought I'd kill two birds with one stone. It may be nothing, in fact, I expect it will be nothing but here I am anyway."

Stella was intrigued but, in her usual style, she didn't push; people always opened up when they wanted to. Stella told her a little about the immediate area around Hilltop and before long they were pulling into her driveway. She got Lizzie's bags from the boot; she left the flowers to sort out later.

"Pretty flowers" Lizzie commented, "as you can tell I do like pink, and these are gorgeous, are they asters?"

"They are, they are for the border at the end of the garden, there's a bit of a tale there but for another time, let's get you settled in."

Stella showed Lizzie to her room.

"Oh, this is magnificent" Lizzie exclaimed, "what a wonderfully calm space and look at that view, that's to die for. How far is it to walk down to the sea?"

"It's a 10 to 12 minute walk down the hill, the pathway is right at the end of the garden, but it's quite a climb back up so if you walk it allow at least twice as long for stopping part way up. So, dinner will be at 7.30, its just you and me at the moment, do you think you would like anything else before then?"

"A strong black coffee with 2 sugars would be perfect, I'll take it here in my room if that's ok? I'd like a shower and a rest before dinner, it's been a long day."

"Of course, no problem, I'll be back in a few minutes."

Stella returned a few minutes later with a pot of coffee, a sugar bowl and a warm pastry. She left Lizzie to settle in and went off to help Marie with dinner.

Marie

Marie was busy in her own world when Stella appeared next to her offering to help chop the vegetables.

"You made me jump," said Marie "I was miles away there, got a few things to think about."

"Sorry" Stella smiled "what's on your mind, is Roger misbehaving again already?"

"No, it's not that, that is going particularly well. He is keeping in touch with Francine, texting etc, arranging their next outing, and I've had my first payment since we talked last week; no, all good there. It's the café, the current owners have sold it and I'm not sure if the new owners will keep me on."

"Goodness, that must be a worry, when will you know? When do the new owners take over?"

"I don't know much about it; Fred, the current owner seems to be keeping the details to himself. He is getting on a bit, so I don't blame him for selling up. I'll have to try and get a bit more out of him this week."

"Let me know what happens," said Stella. She had the seed of an idea, but she needed to think it through much more before she spoke to Marie about it.

"Tell me what went on with your mum and Pete?" said Marie "looked like electricity between them to me."

"Yes," laughed Stella "I think they fell for each other, it's quite sweet really. He gave her a lift to the station today so watch this space, as they say. Today we just have Lizzie, a Scottish lady, she's here for a couple of days, she likes pink, I'll open the pink wine."

"I'm making cottage pie followed by a choice of fruit salad or bread and butter pudding, depending on how healthy she is feeling."

"I'd take a guess that she'll choose the bread and butter pudding," Stella said. She didn't like to judge people, but Lizzie looked like she loved her food and hey, why not?

"Right mon amie, get out from under my feet and I'll give you a shout when its ready."

CHAPTER 39

Lizzie

L izzie was exhausted after her journey and she was grateful for the soft pillow on this comfy bed in this lovely room. She wanted to enjoy her environment, but she was so tired, she just had to have a wee sleep before she did anything else. She set her alarm for an hour's time, she didn't want to be late for dinner and she wanted to have a wander in the garden beforehand.

She woke up with a jolt when her alarm went off; it felt like it had only been two minutes since she had closed her eyes. She lay there waking up and thinking about what she had found out after her mum's funeral. It had been a shock and she hadn't known what to do with the information. Half of her wanted to know everything and the other half wanted to stick her head in the sand and just carry on as if she hadn't ever come across that tatty brown envelope. But here she was, in Cornwall; she wasn't sure what she would find here.

She got up and dressed and unpacked her stuff, then she pulled the tatty brown envelope from her handbag. She emptied the contents onto the bed and took a look at it. She had gone through it all so many times in the last week that she knew it off by heart, but she looked at it again.

She flicked through the newspaper articles:

"4-year-old goes missing from garden"

"Where is Rebecca?"

"No clues in missing girl case"

"Parents plead for any information"

They went on, the articles came and went over a period of 6 months then nothing until a year later when the parents paid for private detectives. There were a few more articles and then nothing.

The next article was 5 years later, about a funeral of Mr Arthur Bartley, where the missing girl was mentioned again as she was his granddaughter.

The other document was a medical certificate for an Elizabeth Claire McDonald, died age 3 from leukaemia. She died at Leicester Royal Infirmary.

Lizzie had done some research into the story of the missing girl online but there wasn't too much to go on as nothing had been online back then. That's why she had decided to come down to Cornwall and see what she could find out on the ground.

Seeing the time, she put all of the old articles back away carefully and pulled on a fleece; she suspected it would be chilly outside. She found her way out to the garden and had a walk around; she found the barn and then had a walk around the borders and found herself standing in the exact spot Rebecca went missing. She didn't know that, but something felt familiar about this spot, maybe it was nothing. She felt a chill suddenly and headed inside to warm up.

Stella greeted her with a glass of rosé and they walked together into the dining room.

"This is an amazing place Stella," Lizzie said, "how long have you been here?"

"Not very long" replied Stella, and she told Lizzie about buying it for a good price and then spending a good nine months refurbishing it before she opened just over a week ago. "It's going well," she said, "I am fully booked pretty much all summer and a good percentage of time this spring too."

"What do you know about the history of this place?" asked Lizzie.

"I have just recently found out a bit more," Stella said, "I can tell you quite a lot about the Bartley's, who owned Hilltop for a lot of years, if you're interested?"

"I'd love to hear about it" replied Lizzie "I love old houses and the history of them, it fascinates me?"

Stella

Stella saw Lizzie standing in the garden from the window, she had just laid the table and opened a bottle of rosé. She wondered what she was really doing here and what the story was that she was researching; she was a long way from home. As she saw Lizzie shiver and come inside, she greeted her with a glass of wine.

"I thought rosé would be appropriate" smiled Stella as she handed Lizzie the glass.

"Absolutely, anything pink is good with me" Lizzie laughed, she was in a pink fleece with pink trainers and her hair was tied back with a pink hairband. "very girly but I've always loved pink since I was a little girl."

"You carry it off," said Stella "let's warm you up with Marie's cottage pie."

They ate the hearty food whilst Stella filled Lizzie in with the Bartley history. She started with Arthur and worked through the family, who was still local, who wasn't around anymore and she told the story of the missing little girl and how that led to the ghost story.

"That must have been devastating for the family," said Lizzie "just not knowing is the worst thing about any situation."

"Yes" agreed Stella "however hard reality is to deal with, not knowing is worse. The worst-case scenario is what always goes through your mind, torture, rape, sex trade, slavery, murder. Murder is almost the best option of those. God knows what that little girl went through."

"And they never found any evidence, no trace of anything?" Lizzie asked, "that's very strange."

"I know, all they found was her doll. She had been playing with it in the sandpit and it was caught in the hedge at the end of the garden."

"What did her parents do?" asked Lizzie "do you know?"

"Well, from what the locals say, they spent years trying to find her; it started with the police and the detectives, then they got their own private detectives. They offered rewards; they spent a lot of money on it over the years but got nowhere. The mother, Jennifer, she always blamed herself and couldn't move on. I mean I don't know how you do move on from something like that, but she did also have a son and it seems that he didn't come out of this too well"

"What happened to him then, did they not pay him any attention?"

"Quite the opposite, they overprotected him so much that he didn't have much of a life outside the house, he must have felt like a prisoner" Stella answered.

"So, what happened to the parents?" asked Lizzie.

"Well, they both died within a few months of each other, he was 76 and she was 68, they say she died of a broken heart. Can you imagine living for 40 years not knowing what happened to your daughter? They also say that she haunts Hilltop, still waiting for her daughter to come home. I haven't seen any sign of anything unnatural in the house but a couple of people have noticed an icy chill in the garden where Rebecca went missing and my mum says she saw her, a shadow in the dark."

"I must say I did feel a chill myself standing at the end of the garden there but I just thought I was cold, which is why I came in and I have to say I have enjoyed this warming meal, thank you."

"You are very welcome, glad you enjoyed it, now would you like fruit salad or bread and butter pudding?"

"No contest," said Lizzie "bread and butter pudding please."

"Coming up" Stella was soon back with a bowl of bread and butter pudding and a large jug of hot custard for Lizzie and a bowl of fruit salad for herself, she had never been a fan of bread puddings.

They enjoyed their desserts and then they retired to the sitting room with a mug of coffee. Stella would clear up a bit later. She was interested to find out a bit more about her latest guest and Lizzie was very happy to chat.

"Tell me about where you live up there in the Highlands, I have never been that far north, I have been to Edinburgh, which is fabulous, lots of history."

"Yes, Scotland is gorgeous, I love living there. I come from a little Hamlet far north of Edinburgh, I have always lived there, well almost. My parents moved there when I was so tiny, I don't remember anywhere else. It is a close-knit community, we always look out for each other and my mum was a district nurse, so she really did know everybody." Lizzie stopped for a moment and looked sad.

"Are you OK?" asked Stella.

"Yes, it's just that my mum died only a couple of weeks ago and I miss her terribly, we were very close, and I moved back in with her a year ago when she got ill. We had some memorable times and it was nice to be with her right to the end. That did give me some comfort, but I just can't believe I will never see her again"

"Tell me about her?" Stella asked.

Lizzie talked about how she had a very happy childhood, her mum always supported her, her dad too but they were never quite as close. It seems there had been some tension at home between her mum and dad and he had left when she was 18. That brought her and her mum even closer together and they became great friends. They would go out shopping together and enjoyed quiz nights at the local pub. Sometimes they would drive into Edinburgh and go to the theatre and have a posh meal out.

Her mum supported her when she went through her IVF treatment and then when she separated and ultimately divorced her husband. Her mum had always been there for her, no matter what.

"She sounds amazing," said Stella gently "it's good to have such great memories of her."

"It is" smiled Lizzie "I was very lucky to have such a great mum. Now I think, if you'll excuse me, I'm going to hit the sack."

"Of course, sleep well" Stella watched Lizzie head upstairs thinking about how lucky she was, herself, to have a great mum. She knew she would be just as sad when her mum eventually passed away. She hoped that that wouldn't be for a long time yet, strong as an ox, her mum would say about herself, and she wasn't wrong.

Stella cleared up the dinner dishes and set the dishwasher running, then also turned in for the night. She looked out into the darkness from her bedroom window... was that a shadow down there in the garden?

CHAPTER 40

Lizzie

Lizzie woke up feeling refreshed and hungry. She had learned a lot yesterday and felt quite at home here. She went downstairs to find Stella laying the table for breakfast.

"Good morning" Stella greeted her "I hope you slept well, help yourself to tea or coffee and I'll have a full English with you very shortly, any special requests?"

"Good morning, I slept well, thank you. As it comes is fine with me, I'm quite hungry this morning" Lizzie sat down and had a mug of coffee and one of the warm croissants that were on the table just waiting to be eaten. Lizzie couldn't resist a fresh pastry, and these were particularly good.

"Oh, that looks fabulous," Lizzie said, as Stella popped a full plate of sausage, bacon, tomatoes, fried eggs and toast in front of her "that will keep me going for a wee while."

"What are your plans for today?" Stella asked.

"Just a bit of exploring, I'd like to get to know the area a bit, nose around the village, walk along the seafront, maybe partake in a coffee and bun somewhere" Lizzie had some very specific exploring she wanted to do but that was her business.

Stella gave her a key so she could let herself back in later on. Stella was popping out for a while this afternoon, but Marie would be there from 4 and Stella would be back later. Lizzie appreciated knowing she didn't have timescales to work to. As long as she was back for dinner at 7.30, which she certainly would be.

After breakfast, Lizzie grabbed her big pink bag and headed off to explore. She took the pathway down and stopped for a moment on the path where it was overlooked by Stella's garden. She looked up at Hilltop, it was quite an imposing house at the top of the hill, then she started her descent down the steep path.

She found herself in the village and had a wander round looking at all the little knick-knack shops, she walked past the local primary school and the small church and graveyard at the edge of the village. She sauntered through the graves until she came across Arthur Bartley; there was a reserved space next to him, presumably for his wife who was still living. Jennifer and Christopher Pine were buried there too. She took a moment to read the gravestones and admire the family plot; the Bartley's were well respected members of the village.

She left the graveyard and explored the little lanes full of terraced cottages, she wondered how many of these were now holiday homes? She hoped that the village still housed mainly locals. She found the street she was looking for; she didn't know the exact cottage, but they were all the same with their stone frontages. Some were in better condition than others, some had flaking paint, she imagined, from the salty sea air. Some had net curtains, but some didn't, and she was able to take a peek into the lives of the people that lived there.

She strolled slowly down the street until she came to the end which brought her to the harbour. She passed the boat shed where she stopped for a moment to watch some sailors push off and head out to sea, then she kept walking until she got to the seafront. She took in all the sights, sounds and smells and when she got to the beach hut café she stopped and bought a coffee and a sticky bun. She sat on the bench overlooking the beach and reviewed her thoughts.

There was something familiar about this place or was it just a beach in general. Her parents had taken her on beach holidays when she was young. This place felt different though, it felt like she knew it. She didn't want to face the thought that was there in her mind. What had started off as an unlikely possibility was turning into a much more likely truth.

She spent the rest of the afternoon pottering about, she had a ploughman's lunch at the pub in the harbour where she struck up a conversation with a few locals at the bar. She wanted to get as much local information as she could, and it seemed people were very happy to talk about old Arthur Bartley and his family. She heard much the same as Stella had told her but hearing it directly from the people that were there at the time had even more impact. She heard the ghost story from several people but no-one that had actually seen the ghost.

Eventually, she decided she had seen and heard enough, and she started that long walk back up the hill. She took it steady and stopped often to catch her breath and admire the view, she was very relieved when Hilltop came into sight. As she walked along the path by the garden, she saw Stella planting in the border there. She went to join her for a chat.

Stella

After Lizzie had left to do her exploring Stella cleared up the breakfast dishes, left the kitchen and dining room clean and tidy and then headed out herself. As she only had one guest at the moment, she was making the most of having a bit of spare time. She decided she was going to go for a hike and had arranged to meet Philip for coffee in the next village at midday. It was a good 10-mile walk to the cafe using the country lanes and pedestrian walkways.

She loved walking, it was such good exercise; she marched briskly to get her heart pumping and had chosen one of her many playlists to listen to on the way. She had tried podcasts, but she found them all a bit tedious and not uplifting enough. She was energised by music and could choose the tunes to suit her mood.

She had her small backpack with her which contained her purse, a bottle of water and her waterproof, you never know when it's going to rain. She hadn't spoken to Philip since Lucy and Grace left, just a couple of WhatsApp messages, so she was looking forward to a catch up. When she got back later, she would plant the asters, it would be good to see the pretty pink and white flowers in the border.

It took her about 3 hours to walk the 10 miles, she had made good time. She could walk 10 miles faster but this walk was over some rough ground and up and down hills so she was happy with that. She arrived at the café at the same time as Philip, he just lived around the corner and so had walked as well. They hugged as they met and went and got a window seat overlooking the manicured garden outside.

"So, stranger," said Philip" How have you been? How were your other guests? How was your mother?"

"You'll never guess what's happened?" Stella said her eyes sparkling "I think my mum is in love!"

"Really," said Philip, "I thought your mother loved being a single woman."

"We all love being a single woman until we meet the right man," Stella said "He was one of my guests, a quiet man who came to paint. He was pretty good. I've asked him to come back and do a painting of Hilltop. Anyway, I think it was love at first sight for him and mum wasn't far behind. He gave her a lift to the station yesterday, so I'll ring her tomorrow and see if he's been in touch since."

"How lovely," said Philip "a bit of romance in the air."

"How about you then?" asked Stella "any sign of romance?"

"No, sadly not, but I am going up to London tomorrow to see Grace. I have a meeting with her team about their approach to marketing to new customers online and I am hoping she will let me take her out for lunch."

"Fantastic" Stella was happy for him "do say hello to her for me."

They chatted over their coffee, Stella filled him in on all that she had found out about the Bartley family, she told him about her guests and about the fact that she was going to have a busy summer.

He brought her up to date on his building work and that it was close to being finished now, he would celebrate with a small dinner party when it was done.

"Do you think Marie would be interested in helping with catering?" he asked.

"Yes, I am sure she would, that reminds me, can I run something past you?"

"Go ahead," he said.

"Well, Marie told me that the café has been sold and she doesn't know yet whether she will still have a job. I have been looking at my booking and accounts and I need some extra help and I think I can afford it, at least in peak season. I was thinking of offering Marie a full-time job, mainly all the catering but she could do the shopping, the ordering and maybe some cleaning as well. What do you think?"

"Well, I think it sounds like a good solution for both of you but you do need to make sure you can afford her all year round, you wouldn't want to have to let her go in the winter months."

Philip wasn't telling Stella anything she didn't know but it was good to have her thoughts confirmed. She would ponder on it a bit longer before she talked to Marie.

"Would you like to join us for lunch on Easter Sunday?" she asked him " I have invited my two friends and Marie and Francine, it would be good if you could come along?"

"I would very much like that, thank you."

They parted company at 2 o'clock and Stella started her walk back. She took the more direct path back and was home by 4.30. Marie was in the kitchen, but Stella wanted to get the asters planted so she said a quick hello and then went straight to the garden shed to get her spade and trowel out. She collected the flowers from the greenhouse and set about planting them, she wanted them to look just right. She had decided she would also put the butterfly stake with them, that would be suitable for the memories of a little girl.

She had just planted the first of the pretty pink flowers when Lizzie arrived at her side.

"Hello there, how was your day?" Stella asked

"Hi, good thanks, I see you are planting the asters? I love asters, those pink ones are gorgeous"

"They are pretty, aren't they? I am planting them as a memorial to Rebecca, they seemed a good choice" Stella looked at Lizzie and saw tears appear at the corner of her eyes then trickle slowly down her sad face.

Stella assumed that Lizzie was thinking about her mum, she was sad about losing her. She stood up to comfort her and heard a very quiet voice say

"I think I am Rebecca!" as Lizzie buried her face in Stella's chest.

CHAPTER 41

Lizzie

Lizzie sobbed quietly in Stella's arms, she hadn't meant to tell anyone, but it had been an emotional day following Rebecca's life around the village and she was now sure that she was Rebecca. She didn't know how or why but she just knew. When she arrived in the garden at the very spot that she went missing all those years ago and Stella was planting the memorial flowers, pink flowers, she couldn't hold the emotion any longer.

She sobbed for a while before she gradually pulled herself out of Stella's arms; she smiled a sad smile at Stella and said "I'm so sorry, I didn't mean to blurt that out to you but standing here feels so familiar, it's like I have been here before. That, and some other stuff I came across when mum died, makes me think ...... " sniff, sob..."...that I am Rebecca."

"Goodness, you poor thing, come here," Stella said as Lizzie accepted the comfort of her embrace again. Lizzie could hear Stella's heartbeat whilst she sobbed.

Lizzie was grateful when Stella said, "Let's go inside, I think you need to warm up. I'll make us both a hot chocolate and then, if you want to, you can tell me all about what you have found out."

She was shivering, although some of that was the adrenaline running through her veins. She would like to talk it through with Stella, she hadn't had anyone to share her findings with and a fresh perspective would be good. She let Stella loop arms with her and they headed inside; she slumped into a chair and waited whilst Stella went and made hot drinks.

Armed with a lovely steaming cup of hot chocolate , Lizzie started to tell Stella about her findings. She explained how she found the box of memorabilia after her mum died and the shock of the contents in the tatty brown envelope. How she had ignored it for days but, ultimately, she had to know so she looked through it all and decided to visit Cornwall. She still didn't believe it, but the thoughts kept nagging at her and being here had brought up some very vague memories.

"Let me get the brown envelope, it's up in my room," Lizzie said. She disappeared returning a few minutes later and emptying the contents onto the floor in front of Stella.

"Here," she handed Stella a few of the newspaper articles, "see, why would she have all these stored away? All these stories about Rebecca's disappearance, they must have meant something to her."

Lizzie watched Stella read through the articles.

"It is strange that she had these" admitted Stella "but it's not enough to mean that you are Rebecca. Maybe she knew the family years ago and followed the story out of interest."

"Yes, I thought that too but then I found this." Lizzie handed Stella the medical certificate confirming the death for one Elizabeth Claire McDonald.

"Woah, well that puts a different perspective on things" Stella agreed "have you followed this up at all?"

"No, not yet. I didn't want it to be true but now I think it's time to look into it and find out the truth. Much as I don't want it to be true there is a family that needs to know what happened to Rebecca, it's just a shame her, ..my parents aren't alive to know about it"

"I also still don't know how I came to live with my mum and dad in Scotland" Lizzie continued "I can't bear to think about some of the possibilities like maybe they bought me through some illegal child fencing ring. I don't have any traumatic memories though."

"What memories do you have that far back?" asked Stella.

"Not much at all, it's more a feeling of familiarity being here. My first real memories are of our garden in Scotland and playing out on the stream that ran at the bottom of it. I seem to remember the beach and playing in the sand but it's so vague, and of course, the house is so different to back then." Lizzie stared out of the window and then back to the paperwork now spread out over the floor.

"What are you going to do next?" asked Stella.

Lizzie paused then answered:

"I have a few things to look into now, firstly I think I'll check out the medical certificate, maybe stop at Leicester hospital on my way back to Scotland, then I need to talk to my dad. I need him to open up to me and tell me what happened back then. That is not going to be an easy conversation."

"No, it's going to be a shock to him that you know about it, take it gently would be my advice and don't jump to any conclusions, just ask the questions."

"We aren't the closest anyway" Lizzie sighed "but, maybe now, I understand why there were tensions in the family; this secret cannot have been easy to live with."

"You sound very calm about it, are you ok?" Stella asked.

"I feel numb at the moment, I have moments of real anger, then sadness, then confusion. Until I know what happened I don't think I will know how I feel. All I know is that my life has been turned upside down after 50 years and I just need to solve the mystery."

"Is there anything I can do to help?" Stella asked "I have some strange sense of responsibility to help solve this mystery. I had already started looking into the family and what happened so I would be very happy to help you with anything you need."

Lizzie was pleased to have Stella's support; she suddenly didn't feel so alone in her quest for the truth.

Stella

Stella couldn't believe what she was hearing, did she really have the missing Rebecca here sobbing in her arms? 50 years since she had disappeared and here she was, maybe, back where she belonged.

She sat and listened to everything Lizzie told her. She looked through the articles her mum had kept and thought that it was strange but not conclusive proof that Lizzie was Rebecca. Then Lizzie showed her the medical certificate of her death and that's when she started to believe that she really could be Rebecca. There was a lot more to find out, of course, but there was a real chance that the mystery of the missing child was about to be solved.

She felt for Lizzie, what a thing to find out; it must have led her to question her whole life. Fancy finding out by chance as well, or had her mum left that envelope there for her to find? Stella could see that Lizzie was in turmoil, she didn't know what to think or feel and Stella also realised that Lizzie now really needed answers, she needed to know what happened and who she was.

Stella offered to help Lizzie, she always liked to help and support people with their challenges, although this wasn't a challenge she had ever envisaged. For this one though, Stella had a real feeling of responsibility. She wanted to be part of solving the Hilltop mystery and hopefully put the ghost to rest.

Since she found out about the missing child, she had wanted to know more about it and to see if the mystery could be solved. She hadn't expected the missing child to just walk into her hotel, but now she was here in front of her, she wanted to help her.

"Maybe we can find out about the death online or by phone rather than you having to go there, then you could go straight from here to visit your father" Stella suggested, she looked at her watch "Goodness, its 7 o clock. Let's take a break and have some dinner, then after dinner, we'll see what we can find out online."

"Thank you, Stella, thank you so much," Lizzie said, "I'll tidy this lot away and take it back upstairs before dinner."

Stella watched Lizzie pack everything except the medical certificate away carefully into its very tatty brown envelope; she left the certificate on the coffee table and took the rest upstairs. Stella popped in to see Marie.

"Hi Marie, sorry I haven't been in to help today, my guest needed some help with some personal stuff."

"No worries, everything OK?" Marie asked.

"Hard to say but she'll open up when she is ready. I'll just go and lay the table." Stella wasn't about to share the news just yet, plus it was Lizzie's news to share when she knew what that news was.

Lizzie and Stella ate quietly. Stella didn't want to babble on about unimportant things unless Lizzie wanted to and it appeared the usually chatty Lizzie was lost in her thoughts. They ate the meal and drank a few glasses of wine. After Stella had cleared everything away, she went and fetched her laptop and they set about seeing what information was available about deaths.

Various websites gave free information about family history including registered deaths, but they didn't find any details of the death of Elizabeth McDonald.

"That's odd, let's look up the birth certificates, do you have yours?" asked Stella.

"Not with me, but yes I do have it" replied Lizzie.

They found the details online which confirmed the birth of Elizabeth Claire McDonald on 16 September 1966 to Geraldine Claire McDonald and Fraser John McDonald at Leicester Royal Infirmary.

"So," said Stella "it seems you were born and died in Leicester, you were only three years old, how sad, but I wonder why the death is not registered online, some admin error maybe?"

They googled "registering a death" and the results showed that when a death occurs in the hospital the doctors complete a medical certificate which is put in a sealed envelope addressed to the Registrar. It has to be presented to the Registrar within 5 days who then register the death.

"What if the death wasn't ever registered?" Lizzie pondered "I still don't understand how they got away with it though, they must have had help from someone."

"I think talking to your dad is the best thing to do next Lizzie," said Stella "he will have all the answers, you never know, maybe he will be happy to tell you."

"Yeah, in my dreams, nothings ever straight forward, is it?"

"You look tired, get some rest and we'll talk again in the morning." Stella didn't think Lizzie would get much sleep, but they couldn't do any more on it tonight.

CHAPTER 42

Lizzie

L izzie tossed and turned all night. She was grateful for Stella's assistance; it had been hard to admit that she was the missing girl. She now felt that she had become a news story, even if it was only her news story. At least she had someone to share it with now rather than dealing with it on her own.

When she did drop off, she had nightmares about being sold at auction to the highest bidder, it was very sordid and dark. It was like a BBC drama and she was the main character, but she never got to the end. Who were her parents? What did they do to get her?

She got up early and texted her dad to ask if she could visit him this week, she didn't say why just that she was down south, and she'd like to see him. Then she sat and wrote a list of questions she needed answers to. She expected him to be shocked that she now knew but it would also be on his mind that, whatever did happen, it was illegal. She would have to tread carefully; she loved her parents and didn't want any backlash for them. She certainly didn't want to taint the memory of her mother.

She packed up most of her things; she was due to leave Hilltop today, but she wasn't sure what she was going to do until she heard from her dad. She would talk it over with Stella at breakfast. It was still early and so she put on her jacket and went for a walk around the garden. Inevitably she ended up standing at the spot where Rebecca went missing and she stayed there for a while just contemplating how life can change so quickly. It was odd, as her life hadn't actually changed at all, but she felt different; she had spent 50 years being Lizzie McDonald and now she found out she was Rebecca Pine.

She heard Stella call to her from the window and so she headed inside and joined her for breakfast.

"Good morning, how are you doing?" Stella asked.

"Not too bad, I didn't sleep much, unsurprisingly, had some dark dreams but I am OK. I texted my dad this morning to see if I can go and visit this week, but until then I am unsure what to do next" Lizzie said.

"Well, I don't have any more guests until tomorrow, so you are welcome to stay another night if you need to" offered Stella.

"Oh, that's great, thank you. I'll see what dad says and I'll let you know if that's OK?"

At that moment Lizzie's phone tinged, and it was her dad.

"He says he'd love to see me and any time this week is fine for him. Oh. now I have to do this"

"That's good news though, grab the bull and all that" Stella encouraged her.

Lizzie finished her breakfast and then looked up train times.

"They go just about every hour from Truro into London it seems. If I get the 10.54, that gets me in at 3.30, and an hour or so to get to dad's. I'll just check he's ok for me to arrive today then I'll get packed."

"I'll drop you at the station," Stella said.

"Are you sure, that's a lot to ask, you have helped me so much already" Lizzie replied.

"Don't be silly, happy to help and you absolutely must call me after you have spoken to your dad."

"I will." Lizzies stomach was tied up in knots at the very thought. "Right, I better get packed up."

She had a lovely text back from her dad to say today was fine and he really looked forward to seeing her. Lizzie wasn't so sure he would feel like that when he found out why she was there, but she would cross that bridge when she came to it. She felt bad for him, but this mystery needed solving.

She finished her packing and went to find Stella; they packed the car up with Lizzies very pink luggage and set off to Truro station.

Lizzie talked through her questions with Stella and they discussed strategy on how to approach the subject in the first place. By the time they got to the station, Lizzie was clear on her plan and she now had over 4 hours on the train to fine tune it.

Lizzie hugged Stella and told her she would be in touch.

CHAPTER 43

Stella

Stella watched Lizzie walk into the station, she watched her until she was out of sight, she looked very alone, and Stella did not envy her the conversation she was going to have with her father. She got back in her car and drove home thinking about this bizarre scenario that had unfolded on her doorstep.

She couldn't tell anyone about it yet, not until Lizzie had all the answers and decided what she wanted to do about it. She was glad she was going to be busy over these next few days with her next lot of guests.

When she got back to Hilltop she plugged in her music and set about giving the place a good clean and tidy. She got all the rooms ready and by late afternoon she was sweaty and grubby, but the house was immaculate.

Stella arranged for Marie to still come today, even though she had no guests, as she wanted to talk to her about her idea. She was just finishing the cleaning when Marie arrived, and they sat and drank a cup of tea together.

"Have you heard any more about the café sale?" asked Stella.

"Yes, it seems the new owners are a family and, at least to start with, they won't be able to afford to employ any staff; they plan to run it all themselves. They take over mid-May in time for the summer holidays, so I have a bit of time to get a new job."

"That's what I wanted to talk to you about, I have had an idea, let me know what you think?" Stella said.

Marie looked interested "Oh, what's that then?"

"Well, looking at my bookings over the summer I am going to need some more help around here and now that I know what my income will be, based on the bookings, I can afford some more help. So, I was wondering if you would consider working here pretty much full time. We could talk about what hours suit us both."

Marie was stunned; she was extremely worried about losing her job at the café and having to go and look for another job somewhere. She loved working for Stella.

"That would be amazing Stella, thank you for thinking of me. What would you want me to be doing?"

"Well, you could take on full catering duties, so, stock, ordering, planning as well as the cooking, then there is laundry and cleaning to do. It would need to be a little flexible as there are times when there are no guests and times when it's really busy. I was thinking that if I paid the salary monthly it would even out over the year, even though your hours may be different each month. That way you know what you have coming in each month."

"And what sort of salary were you thinking of?" Marie asked.

Stella knew roughly how much Marie made between herself and the café at the moment plus she had looked into what local pubs and restaurants were paying their cooks and then taken into account what she could afford.

"I was looking at an annual salary of £18,500" Stella looked at Marie to gauge her reaction and what she saw pleased her enormously.

Marie's face lit up "I think I could make that work," she said.

"Fantastic, we can sort out the finer details over the next couple of weeks. What notice do you have at the café?"

"Well, I am sure they would let me go anytime under the circumstances, but I'd really like to stay and help Fred until he closes at end of the month. That would be about three weeks; would that be OK?" Marie asked.

"Absolutely, I wouldn't expect anything less from you Marie" Stella loved that Marie was loyal to her employer "that gives us time to sort out what hours will work for us, and what it might look like seasonally. I have already thought that I would close in December and January as it won't be busy, and I fancy a break in the sun somewhere."

"That sounds nice," Marie said then drifted off in thought.

"What are you thinking?" asked Stella.

"Well, I always had this dream of running my own catering business and I was just wondering whether in the quieter months you would let me do some small catering jobs from your kitchen? We could share the profit?"

"That sounds like a great plan" Stella was excited about being able to help Marie fulfil her dream and it would also give her some additional income in those off-season months.

They agreed that Marie would start full time on 1 May and they would sort out duties and hours over the next few weeks. It would be a busy summer and then come the autumn they would start to look at catering for some local events.

Stella couldn't be happier; she knew that Marie would be reliable, and it would be great to have the extra help to take the pressure off.

Marie

Marie was ecstatic. She couldn't believe what had just happened, not only had she just got herself a full time job but there was a chance she may be able to meet her ultimate dream of setting up a catering business.

She realised that she was going to have to be flexible with the hours and that the summer months would be manic. Francine was old enough to look after herself now and, at least, she didn't have to worry about money. The salary Stella offered was more than she had ever earned and now that Roger was contributing, she would be able to save some as well. Maybe she would take Francine on holiday in December when she wouldn't be needed at Hilltop.

She wondered whether there might be a few hours work for Francine at Hilltop over the summer; she could make beds with her. Let's not jump the gun she thought, wait until you prove yourself first. Stella was trusting her to be good at cleaning when she didn't actually know, she had only seen her cooking.

Marie wasn't concerned about that; she didn't mind cleaning and would make sure everything was clean. She had got to know Stella, so she knew what standards would be expected.

Marie drove home from Hilltop earlier than usual as there hadn't been any guests to feed. She decided to pop in and see Fred on her way to tell him the good news but also that she would stay on until the end of the month. She had worked for Fred for a few years now and liked him, they had built up a good relationship and she was pleased that he had been able to sell up for a profit.

After a quick chat with Fred, Marie went home to tell Francine her news. She was a good girl really, as good as any 14-year-old is anyway. She found her, as usual, up in her room chatting with her friends online.

"Hi mum, you're early," she said.

"I have some great news; do you fancy a chat?"

"Uh, OK, give me a minute," she said as she went back to talking to her mate "Jules, gotta go, mum wants me, see ya tomorrow."

Marie went downstairs and poured them both some homemade lemonade that they had made together at the weekend.

"So, what's up mum?" Francine asked taking the lemonade.

"Stella has offered me a full-time job up at Hilltop, isn't that great?"

"Oh, yes, great mum" Francine tried to sound interested but she didn't get why that was such a big deal.

"It is great, mon Cherie" Marie told her "as with the café closing, we would have been very short of money and you would have to do without things."

"In that case, yes mum, that's great, well done" Francine loved her mum and wanted her to be happy, but she was a 14-year-old girl preoccupied with her friends and her own life

Marie realised that Francine was suddenly at an age where if she wasn't careful, she was going to be flirting with boys and not understanding about adult life, responsibilities and money.

"This does mean that I will be working longer hours through the summer so I need to know that I can trust you to be grown up and not do anything silly. It means that I will be expecting you to do your homework but also some chores around the place. I will pay you for these as if it was a job."

"How much?" Francine's interest rose; she would be able to buy herself some clothes that she wanted, not chosen by her mum.

"I'll have a think, but I'd like us to work together to have a good life, you up for it?"

"Sure mum, whatever" she sounded like she couldn't care less but Marie could see that she was up for it, she just had to be cool for her image.

Marie smiled at her daughter; it was time to start giving her some life skills. She was very bright, and she was sure she could make something of herself, given the right support.

CHAPTER 44

Stella

Stella was prepared for her next guests. She had cleaned and set everything up yesterday, so she had quite a calm day today. She decided to get out and go for a long, brisk walk along the seafront, first thing, while it was quiet. She threw on her jogging bottoms, polo shirt and trainers and headed out and down the path. She paused briefly as she passed the bottom of her garden, she could see the asters from there and they made her think of Rebecca and Lizzie. She hoped Lizzie's visit to her father went well and she kept her fingers crossed for her.

As she marched down the hill she wondered if Lizzie would want to tell people that she was Rebecca. There was still a family that had been affected by this, particularly Geoffrey and Florence. What would they think about her turning up after all these years?

She arrived at the harbour and turned right to follow the promenade along the beach her thoughts turning to Marie and her agreeing to work full time with her. That was going to be a real help and she knew she could trust Marie to do a great job. She was also really interested in Marie's idea of providing catering for local events in the off season, that could be a little goldmine.

It would be a win win, Marie could make use of Stella's commercial kitchen set up at Hilltop which avoided set up costs. Marie is skilled in cooking and baking and between them, they had contacts they could promote the service to. Yes, she liked that idea a lot.

Before she knew it, she had reached the beach hut café where she spun round and started the walk back. It was a nice 3 mile walk although that hill at the end still wore her out. She stopped at the top and admired the view, she didn't think she would ever tire of it.

She jumped straight into a hot shower when she got back and stood there for quite a while enjoying the water hitting her chilly skin and warming her up. She loved a shower, it always made her feel alive and ready for the day ahead. She dressed in casual jeans and jumper and made herself some granola and yoghurt for breakfast.

Next, she called her mum; it had been three days since her mum and Pete left and she was itching to know if anything had happened.

"Hi Mum" Stella greeted her as her mum answered the phone "how are you?"

"Hi love, I am great thanks, I am just getting ready to go out for the day."

"Oh, nice, where are you off to?" Stella asked.

"I am going to meet Pete in Winchester. Don't you say anything" she laughed "I feel like a schoolgirl again, he makes me feel really special."

"Mum, that's fabulous, I am so pleased for you. I like Pete, he is a real gentleman."

"He is a gentleman, he really is. We have spoken every day since we left your place, but this is the first time we are meeting again. I feel nervous and excited, I have changed my outfit three times this morning."

Stella laughed with her mum "I am sure it will be fine mum, are you getting the train over there?"

"Yes, he's meeting me at the other end. We will have a mooch around the shops and the cathedral and then find somewhere nice for lunch. Listen, I better go love, I'll call you in a few days and let you know how it goes, take care."

And with that, she was gone. Stella smiled at the thought of her mum being nervous; she was always so confident, but she was sure Pete would look after her. She looked forward to hearing about her adventures.

She checked her e-mails and found that her guest due to arrive this afternoon was running late and would be arriving at about 8pm, he hoped that didn't cause any distress. Distress, what a strange word to use. She replied to confirm that no distress had been caused and she would make sure there was a cold supper that he could eat at whatever time he arrived. She texted Marie to let her know that a cold dinner was required this evening, so she could come and do it whenever it suited her.

Stella spent the rest of the day pottering in the house and garden, a bit of tidying here, a bit of organising there. Late afternoon she sat down to read her book for a while and was deeply involved in the story when her phone tinged making her jump.

It was a text from Lizzie.

"Hi, all ok, dad shocked but keen to talk, letting him take his time so staying a few days, will call soon, thx L xxx"

"Oh good" Stella said out loud, then replied.

"Hi, that's good news, thinking of you, take care S x"

Easter

Overall, the Easter weekend went well. Gregory, the Wellness guru had arrived late on Thursday, she had welcomed him in, showed him around and then left him to eat the cold meal provided by Marie and settle himself in. She hadn't taken to him in the short time she spent with him and was glad he wasn't staying long.

It seemed he had booked to see if this would be a good location to bring some clients for a wellness break. He had a good look round at the facilities and the barn and garden and he decided it was "awesome". He admired the "awesome" views and on Friday he did a whistle stop tour of the village, harbour and seafront which were also "awesome".

He was an "awesome" twit in Stella's opinion, but she wasn't about to turn away business. There was a bit of an issue over dinner on Friday evening, but we'll come to that shortly.

During Friday, which was Good Friday two more guests arrived mid-afternoon. Donna and her husband Kev were having two nights away from their 2-year-old son and when Donna had seen that Stella was now running a retreat, she booked it.

Stella had known Donna when she was 18, over 10 years ago; she had joined Stella's team as an apprentice. Stella had quickly learned that Donna was very bright but severely lacked confidence in her own ability. It had been a shame as she was bubbly and outgoing, she got people involved in activities and encouraged other people to take part in projects at work but when she had certain tasks to do, she struggled. Stella had spent a lot of time coaching her back then and they had got on well.

Over the two years they worked together Donna's confidence grew and she became happy to take on tasks and get them done. She still beat herself up when things went wrong but eventually as she matured, she started to learn from mistakes, and this made her better at what she did. She ended up working in graphic design and Stella hadn't seen her in over 5 years.

Donna had some bad family history and it had taken her a long time to let a man into her life, so it was great to see her now as a mother and with a loving and supportive husband. She settled them in and when they came back downstairs, she gave them a glass of wine and they sat and chatted in the sitting room.

Just before dinner, Gregory joined them for a drink, and he told them all about his day exploring. He was a particularly pompous man; he was dressed in a three-piece tweed suit and tie with a coordinated handkerchief poking out of the jacket pocket. He was plump around the middle, he had long hair tidied back in a ponytail and a full beard which was grey in patches. He must have been mid 60s and he had a loud booming voice.

Everyone took an instant dislike to him but acted politely and listened to him talk about his day. Unfortunately, after a few glasses of wine people's tongues loosened and impatience started to show.

Stella, Gregory, Donna and Kev ate dinner together. Marie had made a fantastic beef wellington with all the trimmings and everyone enjoyed the food. As they were finishing the main course Gregory started to talk about how he helped people get over events that happened in their past by introducing wellness methods to their lives. He then started to criticise the Samaritans who he felt were too traditional and made things worse rather than better. He waffled on for ages before Donna couldn't hold back and snapped at him.

"What do you know about the impact they have? Have you ever needed to use such a service yourself Gregory?" she asked.

"Well, no, but I work with people who benefit much more from the whole wellness and positivity approach" Gregory replied puffing his chest out.

"No, thought not, well, let me tell you they are a life saver for some of us, not that you'd understand that with your middle-class opinions."

Gregory continued with his opinionated views of the old-fashioned approach, but Donna was having none of it.

"I am not against new ways of doing things at all Gregory" she raised her voice at him "but some of the old ways are still good and I WILL NOT have a word said against the Samaritans. Those volunteers are highly trained to help people who can't afford help elsewhere, they can't pay the high fees YOU probably charge for your fancy dancy positivity coaching. Let me tell you, I know, they were there for me when my dad's best friend raped me, and my dad stood by and watched. They were there when no one else would listen and I didn't know what to do so don't you tell me what works best."

Donna left the table and Kev followed her with a parting shot to Gregory of: "Well done mate, great stuff."

Stella was left at the table with Gregory who was still sitting bolt upright not quite knowing what had happened.

"Gregory," she said gently "It's often best to keep your strong opinions to yourself when you are with people you don't know. I would have thought in your profession that you would understand that we all have different backgrounds and experiences."

"Well, I didn't think my opinion was that radical, it certainly didn't warrant that response" he said from his high horse.

"Right," said Stella "well, if that is the way you do business, then I am sorry but I won't accept any future bookings from you I'm afraid."

"Hrmph, your loss" he said as he took himself off to his room.

Stella went in search of Donna and Kev and found them cuddled up on the sofa in the sitting room.

"I am so sorry Stella," Donna said, "I didn't mean to ruin the evening, but that man was so, so unreasonable and he wouldn't listen to anyone."

"Don't you worry" replied Stella" I'm sorry you had to go through that. I have told him he is not welcome here in the future and he has gone to his room. He will be gone tomorrow; I'd suggest you have a lie in, and I'll give you a shout for breakfast once he's gone. What an "awesome" arsehole".

The rest of the weekend was great. Donna and Kev had a lovely break and pottered down to the harbour on Saturday. When they got back, Stella's friends Kirsty and Gail had arrived, and they sat around drinking and chatting. They all got on well and had lots in common to talk about. Kev told Kirsty and Gail about the pompous Gregory and now that he had gone, they were able to laugh about it.

"Let's hope you don't get many more guests like that one Stella," said Gail.

"Me too, I know not everyone will be as friendly as my guests so far, but he was just horrible. I decided when I set up here that I wouldn't put up with nasty people, that's the benefit of having your own business surely" Stella replied.

Stella told them all about how she had bought the house and refurbished it and that she was really happy with everything. Donna talked about how she and Kev had met online and hadn't met in person for 3 months because she was so nervous but once they met she just knew he was right for her. Kev was besotted with Donna and their son Ryan.

Gail talked about her three grandchildren and how they were growing up and Kirsty talked about her upcoming wedding and how the plans were coming along. It was a lovely evening and Stella was very happy.

Tomorrow was Easter Sunday. Donna and Kev were leaving early to get back to spend Easter with their son. It had been great to see Donna again and see her so settled and content.

Kirsty and Gail were staying for a big roast dinner along with Philip, Marie and Francine.

CHAPTER 45

Easter Sunday

S tella had got up early to set up an Easter egg hunt around the gardens. Her friends all liked games but mainly they liked chocolate, she was also particularly keen that Francine had fun amongst the adults.

She made an early breakfast for Donna and Kev so they could get on their way and, as she waved them off, she heard Kirsty and Gail nattering on their way downstairs to the dining room. The three of them had breakfast together, it was lovely to have her two good friends to herself for a while.

They sat and chatted and ate and chatted and ate for a couple of hours, catching up on all the news. Stella used to see Kirsty and Gail every weekday at the local leisure centre, they had met there years ago and made friends. They had been a constant in her life for about 15 years now. She hadn't seen enough of them since she bought Hilltop and moved in, but they were always WhatsApp'ing and they had Skype calls regularly.

Lunch was going to be at 13.30 so Stella excused herself to make a start by putting the pork joint in the oven. Kirsty and Gail went out for a walk along the beach and said they would be back by 12.30 which was about the time Stella expected Philip to arrive. Marie turned up with Francine at 12.00 to help prepare the rest of the meal. Francine was a quiet girl but very polite and she was happy to help her mum prepare vegetables whilst Stella focussed on setting the table.

Kirsty, Gail and Philip were staying overnight so Stella had made sure all the rooms were ready. Marie and Francine would get a taxi back so that Marie could enjoy a glass of wine or two. At 12.30 everyone was sitting in the sitting room with a glass of something alcoholic, even Francine was allowed a small glass of wine with a lemonade top.

Kirsty and Gail were introduced to Marie, Francine and Philip and they all got on really well. Stella knew they would, quite different people but all polite and sociable and being Stella's friends, they all wanted to create a nice atmosphere. Marie was keeping an eye on dinner and at 13.35 they sat at the table and enjoyed an Easter Sunday feast of roast pork with all the trimmings, followed by a homemade apple pie washed down with several bottles of wine.

There was lots of chat and, inevitably, the story of the ghost of Hilltop came up. Stella filled in Kirsty and Gail about the tale of the disappearing girl, the grieving mother, the ghost story. She told them all about what she had found out about the family and there was lots of speculation about what had happened. Stella did not mention anything about Lizzie and how the story may unfold but whilst the conversation went on, she did think about Lizzie and wonder how she was getting on with her father.

Stella announced that Marie would be working here full time from May to help her out and then she mentioned Marie's idea of providing catering. Marie went on to tell everyone what she was thinking, her eyes twinkling with excitement at the thought of it. Everyone was very supportive of the idea and offered their thoughts on who their customers might be. Francine surprised everyone by talking through the financials of how it could work, she was obviously a numbers girl. Marie looked on with pride as her daughter held a very grown up conversation about financial planning, risks and contingencies.

Philip offered to help set up the business and get a website up and running when the time came and then decided that it was time to hunt for Easter eggs. Francine's face lit up at the thought of the game, she just hoped she found an egg, she loved Easter eggs.

Stella issued a few loose clues and then set them all off hunting whilst she cleared up and loaded the dishwasher.

Philip

Philip had arrived at Stella's in time to enjoy a few drinks with her friends Kirsty and Gail. He had heard a lot about them over the years but had never met them. Having spoken to them now, he was quite surprised at her choice of friends, not that there was anything wrong with them, they were lovely people. It was just that he always thought of Stella as a dynamic, outgoing risk taker and Kirsty and Gail were, let's say safe and steady. That's obviously what she needed in some friends, he thought, interesting.

Gail was clearly a loving mother and doting grandmother, in her mid-60's, married for over 30 years, she was the mothering friend, the one you go to when you want a hug. Kirsty was mid 50's and about to get married for the first time, after a few failed attempts it would seem. She was your practical friend, knew her HR stuff and loved a good self-help idea.

They were good company and the more he talked to them the more he could see how the friendship really worked for the three of them.

He was enjoying the afternoon but hoped to get a few moments alone with Stella at some point so he could let her know about his trip to London to see Grace. He seized the opportunity when everyone was hunting Easter eggs and Stella was clearing up in the kitchen.

"Hey there," he said, "oops, didn't mean to make you jump."

"Hey, sorry was miles away, how are doing?" she asked.

"Great, thanks. I wanted to let you know the latest on Grace and Lucy if you're interested."

"Oh, yes absolutely, let me just get the dishwasher running and you can give me the low down."

Stella set the washer running and then she and Philip sat at the table with a glass of wine whilst he filled her in on the latest news in London.

"So, I went and met Grace's team and we did some good work on their customer experience strategy and how the website and social media could work better for them. That went well, then I did manage to take Grace for a late lunch which turned into afternoon drinks which turned into dinner and then....... Well, you know."

"No, I don't know, tell me" Stella smiled.

"Well, we hit it off big time and I know I am a bit older..."

"A bit!" laughed Stella.

"Whatever, we had a great time and I ended up staying over at her place."

"You dirty old man" Stella laughed again "how fabulous, was it a one off do you think or will you see her again?"

"I don't think it was a one off. She has been in touch every day since and is planning another trip down here very soon. Grace and Lucy loved it here and Lucy's filming on location is coming to an end, so you'll probably hear from them soon"

"That would be great, and I am so pleased for both of you. I did think you and Grace would be good for each other. My advice, take it easy, Grace is headstrong, and it seems she has a tendency to dive in then runs out of steam quite quickly."

"Yes, I have gathered that, what she needs is a mature older and experienced man to support her and encourage her and one who won't feel threatened by her success. She is a success you know; her company is amazing; her brand is well known and her profit margin is good."

"Yep, sounds like you fit the bill, you old, mature man, you" they both laughed, Philip had never been one to take himself too seriously.

"So, did you hear how Lucy got on with Layla?" Stella asked.

"Well, it seems that her approach worked wonders and not only are they working well together, but Layla is out there on social media promoting Lucy as the best Director she's ever worked with. And, another thing, looks like Lucy and Gary have become an item, take a look at "Hello" magazine, they are all over the front cover."

"Wow, I am so pleased for her, I knew she had the makings of a great Director. She is just young and needs some more life experience; she is one that will just keep learning though. Can't wait to see the film. Now, let's have a look at these piccies of her and Gary."

Stella grabbed her phone and looked up Hello magazine, there they were, holding hands, all dressed up at some film event in London's West End. They made a handsome couple. He looked very comfortable being in the limelight, whereas Lucy had a shy smile on her face, she had only ever wanted to be behind the camera.

Philip was happy to be able to share his news with Stella, he knew she would be pleased for him and Grace, and he was also glad he could update her on Lucy. Stella always wanted the best for people, and he wanted her to know she had played a major part, particularly in Lucy's success with Layla.

"Grace told me that Lucy is so grateful for your advice, it has helped her develop her skills in leadership and in successfully directing the whole crew. Grace told me that Lucy has grown in confidence not just on the set, but in life and that's how she can cope with dating a film star."

"Just happy to help" Stella replied, but Philip could see that she was proud to have been a part of someone's success.

Just then there were screams of laughter coming from the garden, and Stella and Philip went outside to join in the fun. Most of the eggs had been found so now it was time to eat them!

Stella

Easter Sunday was a great success, everyone got on well, the food had been amazing, and the Easter egg hunt worked a treat. Francine enjoyed herself and ended the day chatting seriously to Philip about helping plan her mum's new catering venture. Kirsty and Gail laughed so much their sides ached and, as they were both three sheets to the wind, the laughter came easily. Marie fitted in well this side of the kitchen and was a very proud mum. Philip added an easiness about things, keeping everything light and calm.

Stella had been pleased when he told her about him and Grace and about how well Lucy was doing. She loved to find out how people were getting on and felt happy that she was able to help. She wondered how Jayne was doing; maybe she'd pop her an e-mail tomorrow.

After a fun afternoon Marie and Francine left to go home; they decided to walk as it was a mild evening and Marie said they would benefit from a bit of exercise and fresh air. Kirsty and Gail felt they needed a sit down and so flopped on a chair each in the sitting room, Philip joined them, and Stella made everyone tea.

They were sitting chatting happily when Kirsty announced that she was a bit peckish, everyone laughed but it had now been a few hours since lunch. Stella went and made some sandwiches and when she brought them back in everyone realised they were ready to eat again. After eating Gail helped Stella clear up and then she and Kirsty went up to bed; they were both early to bed people. Stella would see them again first thing tomorrow before they headed home.

Stella and Philip were left chatting when Stella thought she heard a car pull on to the drive; the gravel gave her a warning that someone had arrived. She looked at her watch, 11.15 pm, who would be calling on her this late? She waited expecting the doorbell to go but when it didn't, she looked at Philip.

"I wonder what's going on?" Stella said. She rose out of the chair and went to the front door; as she pulled open the door, she saw a car parked with someone sitting in the driver's seat. The light came on as she stepped out and she saw that it was Jayne, how spooky; she had been thinking about her earlier, but what was she doing here?

Philip had arrived behind her at the door, Stella walked out towards the car and opened the driver's door. She saw a very dishevelled Jayne in floods of tears, mascara running down her face, hardly able to breathe, she was gripping the steering wheel and the engine was still running.

Stella leaned in and turned the ignition off.

"Jayne, what's happened? What are you doing here?" Stella asked gently.

"He, he, he's dead" she stuttered to say through the tears "what have I done?"

Stella looked at Philip.

"Find me a blanket in the laundry room" she directed "and grab the brandy bottle from the kitchen. Whatever's happened she is in shock, I'll bring her into the sitting room."

Philip ran into the house and was waiting there when Stella managed to lead Jayne into the sitting room.

"Sit here" she lowered Jayne into the sofa. She wrapped the blanket around her and held the glass for her to sip the brandy from.

"Take your time, try and breathe" Stella sat beside Jayne holding her, she could feel her shaking.

Jayne started to calm down and she reached into her bag and pulled out a crumpled, damp piece of paper, she handed it to Stella.

Stella opened up the paper and read it.

"Oh my God, Jayne, I am so sorry" she hugged her hard and handed the paper to Philip, it was a handwritten note and it read:

"My dearest Jayne, I love you with all my heart but I can no longer be a burden to you, you deserve a better life and I deserve to be without pain, goodbye my love, John xxxx"

"Jesus" whispered Philip.

Stella sat with Jayne, holding her until she was ready to talk.

CHAPTER 46

Jayne

J ayne had got home from her Pilates class on Thursday; she had enjoyed it. After leaving Hilltop last week she had contacted her friend and they had arranged to meet just before to have a chat. Jayne had committed that she would go every week and was pretty happy that she had been able to, just about, keep up with the class.

John had been supportive when she told him she needed to get a bit fitter and he also seemed to understand that she needed to see her friends a bit more often. She apologised to him for nagging at him to do things he didn't want to do, and she promised to try hard not to do that. She explained that she loved him, and she just wanted the best for him.

When she arrived home on Thursday, she was surprised that there were no lights on; he usually left the outside light on. As she went inside, she couldn't hear any noise, no tv, no music, how strange. She called out and put the hall lights on, no response. Then she saw a slither of light from under his bedroom door, he must have gone for a lie down, she thought.

She opened the door quietly so as not to disturb him if he was asleep. It smelt stale in there, of old sweat and farts. He looked peaceful lying there just lit by the bedside lamp, she walked over to plant a kiss on his forehead when something didn't feel right. She touched him; he was cold. She leaned in but there was no breath. She looked around the room and saw a pill pot rolling on the floor, an empty bottle of morphine and an empty bottle of red wine.

A lone tear ran down her face, she found herself climbing on to the bed and curling up next to him, she held him for the last time. She stayed there for some time before she realised, she would need to call someone. She carefully got up and took one last look at his beautiful face, so calm and peaceful in death, finally without pain and anxiety.

Her business brain kicked in and she called 999, she reported her husband's death to a very kind man, and he promised to send a Doctor round that evening. She got all her documents out, she had an insurance policy that would cover the funeral costs, she found his birth certificate and then made herself a cup of strong coffee whilst she waited for the doctor.

The Doctor and the Police arrived quickly. The doctor confirmed that John was dead by suicide. The police, she established, would need to ensure that there was no foul play. She understood all this and was on autopilot at the moment, not letting her emotions get hold of her. She contacted the funeral Directors who would take the body away and hold on to it for a post-mortem.

Good Friday was not a good Friday for Jayne. There was a lot of paperwork, a lot of people to talk to and a lot of waiting for things to happen. She got through the day and then spent Saturday cleaning. Johns bedroom had been inspected by the police and she could now get everything clean and tidy. She piled all the bedding in the basket ready to wash on Sunday. It was on Sunday that she found the crumpled note, it had got caught inside a pillowcase.

"My dearest Jayne, I love you with all my heart but I can no longer be a burden to you, you deserve a better life and I deserve to be without

pain, goodbye my love, John xxxx"

She read it over and over and then collapsed on the floor in the kitchen, she bawled her eyes out, she screamed, she thumped the floor, she flailed her head backwards hitting the washing machine, she couldn't stop.

What had she done? She had that honest conversation with him and now he had killed himself, for her, so she could have a better life? That wasn't what she meant or what she wanted, she loved him, why would he do this? The thoughts wouldn't stop, never ending circles of random thoughts and emotions.

She didn't know what to do, she had held it together sorting out all the procedures and now she had nothing to keep her mind occupied. Somehow, she found herself in her car, driving, she didn't know where she was going but she had to get out of that house. She had no sense of what time or day it was, but it was dark, and the roads were quiet. She drove and drove, she just kept driving, trying to see through the tears and a few hours later she pulled into the gravel drive of Hilltop. How had she got here?

Stella

Stella sat patiently with Jayne. She had sent Philip to bed, there was nothing he could do to help this evening. Tomorrow there may be things to deal with and he would be good at that, she knew he was there if she needed him.

She watched Jaynes sobs slowly die away as she started to overcome her emotions.

"Are you hungry?" Stella asked her "how about tea and toast?"

Jayne nodded "Yes please," she said in a whisper.

As she ate the toast, Jayne said

"I hadn't realised how hungry I was, I don't think I have eaten today."

"Would you like some more?" Stella asked.

"Yes, please, that would be great."

Stella saw that Jayne had started to perk up a little after eating the warm buttered toast and felt she may be ready to talk.

"Jayne, tell me what happened," Stella asked gently.

Jayne started to talk. She told her everything from when she had got back from Hilltop, the conversation she had with John about needing a bit more time for herself, about not nagging him anymore and expecting more from him, about wanting to get fitter. She told her about enjoying her first Pilates class with her friend and then about how events had unfolded when she got home that night.

"He looked so lovely just lying there, so at peace, I didn't want to disturb that, and I lay with him for a while. He appeared serene and even happy, his face was open; it was like he was smiling and that all his troubles were over. I felt calm and unburdened for a few short moments before reality kicked in and I knew I had to call people.

I called 999 and a very helpful man talked me through what would happen next and that all happened over the next two days, his body was taken to the funeral home and I was left in an empty house. I was dealing with it; I don't think it had sunk in and then as I sorted the washing, I found the note...."

Jayne's eyes welled up and she wiped her runny nose on her sleeve, Stella passed her a tissue.

"and... then it all just got too much, I gave in to the emotions that I had been holding back, I collapsed on the floor with the note in my hand and broke down. I don't know how I got here, I just wanted to get out of the house, everywhere I looked seemed empty without John there. He was always there and now he's gone.

I have so many emotions swimming around in my mind, I feel guilt, loss, sadness, anger, and there is a feeling of relief that then makes me feel more guilty."

Stella just let Jayne talk and open up about how she was feeling, this will be the first time she had said it out loud and that can suddenly make things feel very real.

"I'm so tired," Jayne said "drained."

"Let's take you to bed, I have a room made up, make yourself comfortable and call me if you need anything, any time."

Jayne nodded her thanks and followed Stella upstairs. She had nothing with her so Stella went and found her a toothbrush and toothpaste and an old t-shirt to sleep in. She also got her towels and some clean underwear for tomorrow.

Stella left her to sleep; she had looked exhausted, and she went and quietly tidied up downstairs before heading to bed herself. She, too, felt quite drained; dealing with other people's emotions was tiring. She was asleep as soon as her head hit the pillow.

CHAPTER 47

Philip

Philip had heard Stella put Jayne to bed last night and it had been after 2 am. He wondered what the details of Jayne's husband's death were, but if anyone would help her through it, it would be Stella. She would definitely be the person he would turn to for advice and support and had done over the years.

He wanted to help so this morning he thought he would make a start on preparing breakfast then Stella wouldn't have to worry about it. He was busy in the kitchen when Gail appeared and offered to help him. He gratefully accepted and between them, they found their way around the kitchen to get some bacon butties made.

"What happened last night?" asked Gail, "I thought I heard crying; is Stella OK?"

"Ah, yes. Sorry if that disturbed you. Stella is fine, she had a late-night visitor; one of her previous guests turned up, let's just say, in an emotional state. Stella calmly supported her and then put her to bed. We'll see how she is holding up this morning; seems her husband died a couple of days ago."

"Oh, goodness, no wonder she is upset, but why did she come

here?" Gail asked.

"Well, I don't think she knows but my guess is that she automatically followed the last address in her satnav, and maybe subconsciously she knew Stella was a good shoulder to cry on."

Kirsty arrived at that point and heard the last part of the conversation; she was followed very closely by Stella.

"So, sorry guys, I overslept, but I see you have it all under control, good job you are not paying guests."

"You OK?" Philip asked.

"Yes, fine thanks, it was a late night and quite an emotional one." she looked at her friends.

"I have given them the highlights," said Philip.

"Right, thanks. No sign of Jayne yet? I might just pop up there and check she is OK, you carry on, save me a bacon butty."

Philip watched her head upstairs and decided to be the host; he asked Kirsty to lay the table whilst Gail made tea and he finished off the butties. They had just sat down at the table when Stella returned.

"She is fast asleep, so I'll leave her for now."

Philip led some light-hearted chat over breakfast which the three ladies were all happy to participate in. It was a nice, sociable meal and afterwards Philip offered to clear up so that Stella could chat with her friends before they headed home.

Jayne

Jayne had fallen into bed but, even though she was exhausted, she couldn't sleep, her mind just kept spinning with thoughts and emotions. She tossed and turned but after an hour or so she got out of bed. She went to the bathroom, had a wee, washed her face and then went back to the bedroom and stood looking out of the window. The moon was bright, the sky was clear and she could see the lights of the harbour.

She suddenly felt chilly and as she turned away from the window, she was sure she saw a shadow down in the garden, she looked out but there was nothing there. She remembered the story of the ghost and the missing girl as she got back into bed. How would you cope with never knowing? At least she knew. She fell into a deep sleep dreaming of her love, her John.

When she woke, she was surprised to feel a lot better, she checked the time, 10.20 goodness, she had slept well in the end. She took a long shower and pulled on the underwear that Stella left out for her and yesterday's clothes. She always carried some basic make up in her handbag which she applied. She checked herself in the mirror, she looked presentable enough.

She went downstairs in search of coffee and found Stella and Philip sitting chatting at the table.

"Good morning," she said, "I just want to say thank you for looking after me last night. I was a right mess and I am so sorry for just arriving here like that."

"Don't worry," said Stella "we were happy to help; you look a lot better today. Coffee?"

"Coffee, yes please, lots of it."

"Let me introduce Philip properly," Stella said.

"Hi, yes, we did meet briefly when I stayed here; you came to fix some web site problem didn't you?"

"I did, yes. It's good to see you again and looking so well this morning. Is there anything we can help you with today?"

Jayne was feeling pretty good today and was thankful to have found such lovely and helpful people to be with.

"Thank you, but I will be fine now, meltdown over" Jayne smiled "I will have to call the police about the note and then

I have lots of people to contact to let them know about John's passing. Once they have the post-mortem results, I will be able to get the funeral arranged. Another step in the grieving process."

"I do have a favour to ask if it's possible?" Jayne looked at Stella "if the room is free would I be able to stay tonight as well? I love it here, it's so calming, and I have nothing to go back to. Obviously, I will pay, for last night and tonight."

"Yes, absolutely, the room is available. I have some other guests arriving from Wednesday onwards, but I am not fully booked until the beginning of June."

"Great, thank you." Jayne said "I may have to go and buy myself a few things" she laughed looking at her only outfit.

Jayne accepted the offer of a full English breakfast; all these emotions were making her hungry and that healthy diet had gone out of the window for now anyway. After breakfast, she drove to the nearest big town and bought herself a few items of clothes and ablutions. Then she headed back, parked in the village and had a long stroll along the seafront. She stopped at the beach hut café for a ploughman's lunch and sat and watched the world go by. She might stay on for a few days if Stella had the room free. She loved it here

Every now and then she would well up and have a little sob when she thought about John. Everything would bring back memories of the good times that they shared, and she would flick between smiling and crying. The later years of their relationship had been hard, but they still experienced some laughs and good times and it would be weird to think of life without him.

She started to think about that; life without him, what would she do? She guessed she would carry on, go back to work and settle into some normal routine. Financially, she was doing fine, she had a good job, no mortgage and some significant savings.

John took out life insurance after his accident, but she wasn't sure it paid out for suicide, she'd have to check at some stage.

Did she want to carry on in this normal routine? She had always wanted to travel more, maybe she should do that? But doing it alone, that's not the same at all. Hum, maybe she would stay at work and splash out on posh holidays, hire a villa in the sun, that sort of thing.

She spent the whole day out and about with her thoughts, enjoying the hospitality of the villagers, pottering around the shops and buying a few items here and there. She drove back to Hilltop; she wasn't about to attempt the hill today and she still had her car with her. She got back just as the sun was starting to drop, it was 18.30 and she was looking forward to a chat with Stella over dinner.

She met Stella in the hallway who greeted her.

"Hey, Jayne, come on in, would you like a glass of wine? Let me introduce you to Lizzie"

CHAPTER 48

Lizzie

Lizzie had called Stella first thing Monday morning and asked if she could stay for a couple of nights whilst she got all her thoughts together. Stella had been pleased to hear from her and confirmed she had a room available for a few nights. Lizzie hadn't told her much on the phone as she would rather tell the whole story in person. She had booked a ticket on the 11.22 from London Waterloo which arrived in Truro at 16.18. That gave her time to have a last breakfast with her dad before she left.

She sat on the train thinking about the last few days. A lot had happened since she left Hilltop only 4 days ago. Her dad had been amazing, they worked through things together and he told her everything.

He was really pleased to see her when she arrived, and they had a good catch up. He was sorry about her mum's death and apologised for not coming to the funeral, but he couldn't face seeing all those people again after so many years. That opened up the opportunity for Lizzie to mention the tatty brown envelope that she found. She took it out of her big pink handbag and gave it to him to look through.

His face went pale when he saw what was in there; he had no idea that her mum had kept that stuff. Lizzie assured him that she wasn't angry just curious, and she wanted to understand what had happened. She explained that she was unsure of her life and who she was, and she just needed answers.

It took her father a while to get over the shock and she didn't get the answers she wanted that first evening. She didn't push him, she had the time and she could see that he was not sure how he was going to tell his daughter the truth, where he would start.

The next morning, they had sat and talked, really talked and it took most of the day. This is his story:

"Your mum and I lived in Leicester, we both worked at the hospital, she was a nurse and I was a technician, that's where we met. We were very happy together and were so excited when she fell pregnant. We had a gorgeous little girl called Elizabeth, we called her Beth, who we doted on. We were so upset when she was diagnosed with Leukaemia, watching the poor little thing go through the treatment was hard but then, when we were told she wouldn't survive, we were devasted. We both sat by her bedside in her last weeks; we tried to make her comfortable and let her know she was loved. She was 3 years, 4 months and 8 days old when she died.

Our world was shaken, we were both grief stricken. Our managers at work were really good, they gave us the time we needed to grieve and get ourselves back on our feet. Things were a struggle emotionally; no-one should outlive their children. We both went back to work, but your mum was so sad. I was sad too, but it hit her hard. I guess being the mother you have that extra connection.

After about 4 months I booked us a weekend away in Cornwall. I thought it would be good to have a change of scenery. We stayed in a static caravan by the beach and went out for walks and pub meals; it was nice, and your mum seemed to enjoy it. Taking her away from the haunting memories did seem to lighten her mood a little.

We were out for a walk one day and we'd taken the walk up the hill from the harbour, just exploring a new path and enjoying the amazing views. I got to the top and realised that your mum wasn't behind me anymore, I turned to see her disappear round the bend in the path heading back down. I figured she had run out of steam and decided to walk back down the hill, so I quickened my pace to catch up with her.

She was almost at the bottom when I caught up with her and I saw that she was carrying a little girl, they were talking and laughing together. I asked her what was going on and she put the girl down and introduced me to Lizzie. She looked at me with a sparkle in her eyes and told me Lizzie was our daughter now. Of course, I couldn't let that happen, I didn't know where this little girl had come from, but she wasn't ours, plus she kept telling us her name was Rebecca. She was 4, she knew who she was, but she seemed happy enough.

Suddenly we found ourselves back at the caravan park and your mum was so happy. I hadn't seen her like that for months now, I thought a couple of hours playing with the little girl wouldn't do any harm and then I'd take her somewhere and find out where she belonged. I told your mum that was what we would do, and she agreed, well, she didn't disagree.

I went to get us all some fish and chips and when I came back your mum had gone, packed up, taken the car and the little girl and gone. No mobile phones back then, so after sitting for a bit and considering my options I decided to hop on a train and head home, that would be the only place they would go.

I was furious when I got home. Your mum was there with the little girl, let's call her Lizzie, that's what your mum called her, sorry, you. I told her, she couldn't keep you, you were not our daughter and some other poor mother would be worried sick. She wasn't having it, she had gone mad, she was keeping you and I could like it or lump it. She had a plan, we would move to Scotland, our name was McDonald after all, we would fit in there, get new jobs, leave Leicester and everything we knew behind us to start a new life with you, our stolen little girl.

I am not proud of what we did, but we did it. We handed in our notice at work; we found a house to rent in the Highlands whilst we sold our house in Leicester and we moved lock, stock and barrel to Scotland. Neither your mum nor I had any living parents or siblings or none that we were in touch with, anyway, so it was only friends we left behind. Friends don't track you like family would and so we just disappeared from our old life.

You were an amenable child, your mum told you that you were staying with us for a while as your own mum was poorly. There were a few tantrums and screaming for your mum but, overall, you settled in pretty easily with us.

It seems that your mum never logged the medical certificate of Beth's death with the registrar and with us leaving the area no-one ever followed it up, so her death was never officially and legally registered and we just used Beth's documents for you. You were a little older but not enough for anyone to question it.

We were living in a very small hamlet in the Highlands and they took us in and made us welcome. Your mum got a job easily as a part time district nurse and I got work at the nearby factory fixing their machinery. We made a comfortable living between us and life would have been good.

But I struggled to live with what we had done. I didn't follow any news; I didn't want to know what had been reported. Your mum became her old self again, lively, bubbly, supportive, the perfect mum but all I saw was a child abductor. You may have felt some tensions at home, that's why. I made a promise that I would stay and support you both until you were 18.

I did that and then I left, I got as far away as I could and moved to London. I love you, have always loved you as a daughter, but I hope you'll understand that you were not my Beth. It's not your fault and so I never blamed you or let it affect my love for you but what we did, it's just not right.

I am so sorry that you have found out the way you have, and I beg your forgiveness for what's happened but I, for one, am glad that it's not just my secret anymore.

There is one more thing I need to tell you. Completely by chance, I came across your birth brother Geoffrey Pine a few years ago. He lives and works in the City as a trader. I was in the dentists' waiting room reading one of the magazines they had lying around, and it had an article in it about the trading floor and the stock exchange. Geoffrey was one of the people they interviewed, it gave the name of his company and so I went and bought a few shares from him. He was basking in the limelight of the article and didn't seem suspicious. He was a typical, sleazy trader I'm afraid. Anyway, I kept a loose track of him, and I know where he lives if you did want to get in touch with him."

Lizzie listened intently as her dad told the story of her abduction; she had lots and lots of questions which he patiently answered as best he could. They stopped to eat at some stage then came the big question: what to do next? Did she want to meet Geoffrey and the other members of the Bartley family? What would happen? Would her dad get arrested? How would her life change?

Lizzie and her dad talked through all the options and scenarios. They decided not to do anything in a rush; it had been 50 years, it could all wait a bit longer. All Lizzie knew was that she didn't want her dad to get into trouble, which he would if the truth came out. She felt that she should be angry with her parents and the occasional rage surfaced but she loved her parents so much, they had been her parents for 50 years and had given her a good life.

The train sped through the countryside, but Lizzie didn't see it, she was in her own world. She had spent some quality time with her dad over the few days she was there and had got to understand how hard his life had been, always looking over his shoulder wondering when they would be caught and she would be taken away. It still didn't excuse what they had done but that wasn't her fault and she didn't want her life torn apart.

She would talk it through with Stella, she was the only other person in the world that knew her secret.

CHAPTER 49

Stella

Stella spent the morning clearing up after everyone had gone. Kirsty and Gail had left by 9 am, Philip hung around until after Jayne had gone for her walk and helped her clear the plates to the kitchen, then he left and she found herself alone for a few hours before she picked Lizzie up. She was pleased that Lizzie had called her this morning, in fact, that's what woke her up. She was looking forward to finding out what her father had told her, she hoped that Jayne stayed out so that she and Lizzie had some time to themselves.

Marie would arrive at 4 pm, as usual, to cook for her and her two guests so that left Stella free to deal with cleaning, laundry, admin and of course, taxi duties.

She thought about Jayne as she was loading the washing machine. What a shock to arrive home and find your husband had killed himself. She knew that Jayne was feeling guilty about it. That would take some time to subside, but deep-down Jayne was feeling relief and that was the hardest to come to terms with. She wondered what Jayne would do with her life now, perhaps that was what she was thinking through whilst she was here away from it all.

She sat down with a cup of tea and a sandwich before she went to pick Lizzie up from the station. What a couple of weeks it had been. She always knew she would meet interesting people running a retreat, but she never expected the drama that had unfolded.

The traffic was heavy on the way to Truro station; lots of people driving home after the bank holiday weekend. She pulled up just as the train did and waved at Lizzie, you couldn't miss her in her glory of pinkness. Lizzie ran over and got in the car out of breath.

"Hey" she panted.

"Hey yourself" Stella replied "how are you doing? Lots to tell, I hope?"

"Indeed" and Lizzie started the tale on the drive back.

When they got back Lizzie dumped her stuff in her guest room and joined Stella for a glass of wine. They sat looking over the sea and Stella listened to the whole story without interrupting. What a sad story, two families affected by the loss of a little girl. Both mothers now passed away and families moved on with their lives, just leaving one not so little girl coming to terms with what had happened.

Stella watched Lizzie as she talked, she was very calm about it all; she guessed she had got most of the emotion out when she was with her father. She wondered what she was going to do now.

"How do you feel now you know the truth?" Stella asked.

"Well it's weird. I thought I'd feel angry, really angry at what my parents did, and the fact that I am not who I thought I was, but you know... I am Lizzie McDonald, I have been for 50 years and I still am. This sad tale doesn't change that, to me; I don't remember that life, that little girl. I have had a great life; I still have a great life and that's what my parents gave me."

"What about the Bartley family; do they deserve to know?"

Stella asked.

"I don't know" sighed Lizzie "I know I should want them to have closure but do I want all that fuss? Do I want my dad to go to prison for giving me a good life? I really don't know."

"Your dad did do wrong, you know Lizzie, he and your mum did ruin another family."

"I know, I do realise that, and I know that's the right thing to do for them but is it right for me? Rebecca's mum and dad are both dead, her brother has moved on, I don't know how close her uncle and cousins were and the only person that is likely to care is the grandmother Florence and from my research, she is suffering from dementia. So, who is going to benefit from the truth?"

"I know what my parents did was despicable" Lizzie continued "but my mum is dead, and my dad has spent his whole life beating himself up about what they did. It feels to me that there will only be losers if the truth comes out."

"This is a big decision Lizzie," Stella said, "take some time to think about it, maybe over another bottle of wine?"

Stella had been taken off guard at Lizzie's thoughts on, maybe, not telling people the truth, she had just assumed the mystery would be solved and the Bartley family would get closure. You should never assume and as she went and fetched another bottle, she started to see the logic in Lizzie's argument. She was sure they would talk more tomorrow, but she had just seen Jayne arrive back and so she invited her to join her and Lizzie for a drink.

Lizzie

Lizzie could see that Stella was surprised at her not wanting to share the truth and had asked some good poignant questions. That is why she wanted to talk it through with Stella before she made a final decision; her dad knew she needed some time to process things. Stella would push her into thinking about things she didn't want to face but wouldn't force anything on her. She trusted Stella completely and knew that whatever her decision was, Stella would support her.

They had a good couple of hours together; Stella had listened without butting in and then asked her questions at the end. Lizzie knew what the morally correct thing to do was, but she had found all the arguments against doing that and, in her head, it sounded reasonable. Why should she lose everything she had? Technically she was the victim in this story? She didn't feel like a victim and didn't want to be the victim, she also didn't want to be a news story.

Stella was right, it's a big decision; she would take her time to think it over some more. She saw Stella return with not only a bottle of wine but with a guest. Stella introduced Jayne.

"Lizzie, this is Jayne, she is staying for a couple of days after a very sad event; she can tell you about it. Jayne, this is Lizzie. I'm going to leave you together to chat if that's OK, whilst I help Marie get dinner ready. I'll be back in a bit."

Lizzie stood up and shook hands with Jayne.

"Pleased to meet you Jayne, would you like a glass of this fine wine?"

"That would be perfect, thank you." Jayne accepted the glass and asked, "Whereabouts in Scotland are you from?"

"Ach, you noticed the accent hey?" Lizzie said in her broadest Scottish accent "Way up in the Highlands lassie, what about you?"

"Oh, home counties, very ordinary," said Jayne "but I love it here by the sea, I find it very therapeutic, nothing seems a problem when I'm here."

Lizzie saw the sadness in Jayne's face and went and sat next to her.

"Now, lassie," she said taking her hand "let's have a drink and you can tell me all about it."

Lizzie let Jayne relax and share her grief with her. She listened to her talk about her John and how she had found him just a few nights ago. She listened to her share her innermost feelings for him and how their lives had changed after the accident. She listened to the exciting adventures they used to have and laughed at the funny stories she told about their travels.

When Jayne had shared enough about her loss, Lizzie then talked about her feelings for her mum. It was still only a few weeks since her mum had passed away and listening to Jayne had reopened some of her own grief. She spoke about how she had nursed her mum in her last year and how they enjoyed each other's company. They had been best friends and it had left a huge hole in her life now she was gone.

Lizzie liked Jayne. They had only just met but it felt like they were kindred spirits, they were dealing with some of the same issues in their lives, she was keen to get to know her better. She wasn't about to divulge her secret though, not until she had decided what to do.

Stella

When Stella went to fetch Jayne and Lizzie for dinner, she found them cuddled together on the sofa giggling like schoolgirls. She smiled at the sight of them, the worse for wear after quite a lot of wine being drunk.

"Come on ladies, time to sober you up with some homemade fish and chips," Stella said.

"Oh lovely" they both looked up and then followed Stella into the dining room. Stella knew both of these ladies enjoyed their food and thought that good old traditional fish and chips would be appreciated. And there was sticky toffee pudding for dessert, one of Stella's favourites with lashings of hot custard.

"So, you two have got to know each other a little then?" she asked knowingly.

"We have" replied Lizzie "it seems we have a lot of the same issues going on at the moment..."

"And a lot in common" added Jayne "in just a couple of hours we have become good friends."

"It must have been meant to be, us two coming back here spur of the moment if you like," said Lizzie.

"Well, there was certainly no planning involved" laughed Stella "but I am a big believer that people often turn up in your life just as you need them. What plans have you both got now then?

"Well, I have a few things to sort out with the police and organising the funeral. I also need to let work know that I won't be back for a little while, they will be fine, they are very supportive. Then I have to decide what to do with the rest of my life – just a small thing," Jayne shared.

"And for me; I, also, have a few things to address. I promised to talk to my dad again soon; I have two weeks booked off work, so I still have a week left. I, too, then need to think about what I want my future to be. I don't have anything in Scotland, just a few friends, and I would love to travel and write" said Lizzie.

"Well, looks like you both have a bit of thinking to do, maybe you could go travelling together?" Stella suggested, it was a bit tongue in cheek, they had only just met but she threw it out there.

Stella saw Jayne and Lizzie take this idea in and look at each other; nothing was said but she suspected they were both weighing the idea up before either committed to anything at this stage.

They had a lovely, sociable dinner with a few tears now and then when John was mentioned, and Lizzie still had sad moments talking about her mum. Overall, though, it was very pleasant and very drunken. Three bottles later Jayne and Lizzie both headed up to bed, leaving Stella to clear up.

CHAPTER 50

Stella

Stella was, as usual, up early preparing breakfast when Lizzie joined her.

"Morning Stella," said Lizzie. Stella knew immediately that Lizzie had made a decision and wanted to share with her.

"Morning Lizzie. You look like you have something to tell me?" Stella smiled at her putting her at ease.

"I have, I thought long and hard after we talked yesterday and I have decided that, at least for now, I am not going to tell anyone that I am Rebecca. I am going to keep my life normal; I am going to remain Lizzie McDonald and keep my dad safe. I know all the arguments, but I have to think about what's best for me and my family. I know I don't need to ask but please, please, keep this to yourself. You are the only person that knows the truth and I need to be sure that it stays that way" Lizzie looked at Stella with pleading eyes.

"Of course," Stella looked at her "if that's what you want, it's your story and your life, I wouldn't do anything to ruin that. I get it and respect your decision."

"Thank you so much. Now I must go and put my dad out of his misery and let him know" Lizzie went to call her dad before breakfast.

Stella watched her go and sat down for a moment to take it in; she did get it. From an outsiders view it would seem obvious to tell the truth and not live with that secret. But from Lizzie's point of view, there was nothing to gain by telling the truth and solving the mystery. It can't have been easy to make that decision and Stella admired her for being strong throughout this discovery.

Lizzie and Jayne

After a hearty breakfast, Jayne and Lizzie left Stella to get her rooms ready for her next batch of guests arriving tomorrow. They put their raincoats on as the sky was heavy and they walked down the hill into the village. While it was still dry, they walked along the prom, past the beach hut café and as far as they could go before turning back and retracing their steps to the village.

They pottered around the shops together, admiring the same things and treating themselves to some Cornish fudge. When they got to the book shop, they gravitated towards the travel section and started flicking through city guides and European train journeys.

"Where would you go if you could go anywhere?" Lizzie asked Jayne.

"Oh, so many places. I love Europe and would go back to Italy tomorrow, but I have never been to Australia and I'd love to go and visit the Gold Coast. How about you?"

"Australia for me too," Lizzie said, "I love the thought of being a beach bum on Bondi beach."

They looked at each other.

"Should we do it?" Lizzie said out loud.

Jayne laughed "Tell you what let's buy a book on Oz and go and talk about it over a pub lunch."

"Great idea" Lizzie picked up two books and they paid and went looking for the pub.

On the way they stopped and looked in the different shop windows including an estate agent, everyone loves looking at houses, don't they? They picked up a local property paper from the basket outside and took it with them to the pub.

Over a pub lunch and a Cornish cider, they chatted and looked through the books on Australia. They dreamt about what their ideal trip would be. Maybe a camper van trip across the outback or maybe a villa on the beach. They sat and planned; even if was only a dream, the planning was fun, and they filled a couple of hours sitting in the pub.

"Do you know what I'd really like to do?" said Jayne "I'd like to write a novel. I've always wanted to but just never had the time. I always imagined myself, one day, sitting looking at the sea and writing some crappy romantic novel."

"Well, you should do it." said Lizzie "Do you need to work? Do you need that 9 to 5 job you have always had?"

"I don't need it and I am not looking forward to going back. I love it here so much; I could just stay and leave everything else behind" Jayne realised that she meant that.

"Then, that's what we'll do." Lizzie said, "Pass me that property paper."

She turned to the lettings sections and browsed to see what was available.

"Here we are," she said "2 bed cottage to rent, summer season, all bills included, £2000 per month. Let's go and see it."

"What?" laughed Jayne "now?"

"Why not, come on, you grab the bags, I'll pay the bill."

THE END

ABOUT THE AUTHOR

Sheila Starr

Sheila lives in Eastleigh on the South Coast of England with her husband. She has worked in corporate life for over 30 years managing customer service and transformations teams. She has spent a lot of time coaching and mentoring and now runs her own coaching business.

When work was slow during lockdown Sheila decided to fulfil her dream of writing a book. This is her first book but she hopes it is the first of many.

Printed in Great Britain
by Amazon